I Was A Teenage Angel of Death

An Unrequited Love Story

Robert Dwight "Buddy" Brown

Allonymous Books
A Division of Chi Xi Stigma Publishing Company, LLC

ISBN 13: 978-1-931608-77-0

Copyright©2017 Robert Dwight Brown
Republished in a new edition 2025

Previously published as Teen Death Angel *on Kindle Direct Publishing* ©2015

"art deco frame vector: Freepik.com." The title pages were designed using resources from Freepik.com

Publisher's Note: Because of the nature of the writing assignment made by Mrs. Story to her students Buddy Brown, Sarah Sue Hayes, and Eugene "Johnny Angel" Clark, the author has intentionally left spelling and grammatical errors in this manuscript to create a feeling of authenticity to the stream-of-consciousness writing the high-school students are to write in their diaries- nay- journals. The typesetter has done his best to maintain the vision of the author.

The mind is a patchwork of yesterdays,
Blurring together as the memory decays.
One by one turning cloudy and gray,
And into the ether they soon blow away,

I wouldn't change how my life was written,
But there was another time when I was smitten,
With the girl from next door, my best friend,
And I thought I knew how my life would end.

But when I think of Sarah Sue Hayes,
All the years seem to fade into days.
Back when the future was a distant someday.
Ah, I remember it like it was yesterday.

I knew God would answer my prayers,
To make Sarah Sue and Buddy the perfect pair.
That's how it would be if I was the author of my life,
I'd be the perfect husband, Sarah Sue'd be my wife.
(Chorus)

The mind is a patchwork of yesterdays,
Blurring together as the memory decays,
One by one turning cloudy and gray,
And into the ether they soon blow away.

Malt Shop Records

BUDDY BROWN & SARAH SUE
I WAS A TEENAGE ANGEL OF DEATH

SIDE A

1. LIKE IT WAS YESTERDAY
2. THE GIRL NEXT DOOR
3. THE GIRL NEXT DOOR - PART 2
4. WHY DO GOOD GIRLS LOVE BAD BOYS?
5. THANK GOD! GOOD GIRLS LOVE BAD BOYS!
6. DADDY'S ANGEL

I met her on my birthday,
The year that we turned four
I was new to the neighborhood,
She was the girl next door.

My mom invited the neighborhood.
But the sun was shining clear.
My "friends" played in their yards
She was my only guest that year.

    Friends forever, friends forever,
    Nothing will tear us apart.
    Friends forever, friends forever
    I'll always have a little piece of her heart.

There was a rainy day,
The year that we turned six.
I went over to play doctor,
He didn't even know he was sick
"I promise to show you mine,
If you show me yours."
He blushed bright red
He'd never played doctor before
    (Chorus)
      (change pronoun)

Then on Easter Sunday
The year that we turned seven
I promised to be her friend,
Until the day I entered Heaven,

Her daddy didn't let her
Have any friends over to play.
I had a set of walkie-talkies,
And we'd talk night and day
    (Chorus)

Before our first Eucharist
The year that we turned nine
I made Buddy, good honest Buddy
Steal a bottle of Communion wine.

We got drunk for the first time
On the blood of Emmanuel.
Buddy feared for our souls,
Said we'd both go straight to hell
    (Chorus)

        We'd both go
        Straight to Hell.

Like It Was Yesterday

"Welcome to the Malt Shop radio hour," the disc jockey said, "where we play all the greatest hits from that by-gone era, the 1950's; when life was all about cruising Main Street on a Friday night with your girl beside you in your Chevrolet, and stopping by the car-hop burger joint for a quick bite. Not this constant fear of the Vietnam war looming over our heads, sending our young men to their deaths. The 1950's were a time of constant employment and the fear of the great red dragon, Communism, was in its infancy. I like to look back on those days, those brighter, sunnier days and remember life when I was a child after the war, rolling-skating down the street without fear, to my days as a disc jockey spinning wax every Friday night during the Malt Shop hour. I had the great pleasure of discovering several good singers and a couple of really great ones.

"Tonight, we will relive one of those 1950's moments from 1957. Not as sunny as most, let me tell you, but a story that has to be told and a story that has to be remembered. It is one heck of a good story, my listening audience.

"Buddy Brown, the singer-songwriter, has re-released his long out-of-print debut masterpiece *I Was A Teenage Angel of Death* to wide critical acclaim. It's shooting up the pop charts as we speak. We have him here tonight to talk a little about that landmark recording and play the cuts from that album, including a few new songs recorded particularly for the re-release.

"Here he is- Buddy Brown."

"Thank you, Mr. Perkins."

"Soda Jerk."

"Sorry. Thank you, Soda Jerk Perkins. Thanks for having me," I said.

"Our pleasure, Buddy. Our pleasure. You came onto the scene in 1957 with *I Was A Teenage Angel of Death* and immediately became an unlikely teen idol."

"Unlikely is an understatement."

"You had those dorky glasses and trademark cow-lick and all the girls just seemed to swoon all over you."

"That was quite a shock to the system. I'd always been very unlucky in love. All the girls at my high-school never gave me a second glance. But once I recorded *I Was A Teenage Angel of Death* and went out on tour to support it, well, it was quite a shock to the system. I already said that, I'm sorry. But it was. I always dreamt that girls would throw themselves at me like Elvis Presley and faint in the aisles like they eventually would for the Beatles. When I finally came up on that stage and sang my first number, heck, it would like a thunderbolt striking all those girls at the same time."

"It must have been quite a good feeling."

"For a nerd like me, it was vindication. The girls loved me in spite of my glasses and my cow-lick. Like you said, it became my trademark. My calling card if you will. I've given it all up now, of course. It's a different age and a different era. Being a teen idol is fine when you're young, but as you age, things change and you have to grow musically or you'll just die."

"You've embraced the singer-songwriter style of music now. Why?"

"Singer-songwriters have an honesty to them. Back in the 50's you could rock 'till you dropped and throw in a few ballads here or there for the girls, but teenagers back then wanted something that would shock and horrify their parents. Rock 'n' Roll gave them what they wanted most. Sure I was singing black music to white teenagers, but by the time that I came around, Rock 'n' Roll was all the rage. Now that I'm older and more reflective, I like the simplicity of one man and his guitar. There is something so Zen about it. So peaceful."

"Why record a Rock Opera. Today, we think nothing about it. The Who did *Tommy*, but back in the 1950's it was unheard of.

"I never thought of *I Was A Teenage Angel of Death* as a Rock Opera. Pete Townshend was the first to come up with that concept. I just wanted to tell a story on a duet album. Just me, Buddy Brown, and a lovely singer to play the part of Sarah Sue and a crooner to sing Johnny Angel's part. Sure it told a story, but I never thought of it as an opera. It was just a series of songs and duets that would immortalize my first love, Sarah Sue."

"And you've never forgotten about her, have you?"

"You don't forget your first love no matter how much it hurts. You just can't forget. It's like God is cursing you with this vibrant memory. The more painful it is, the more vivid the memories are. You sometimes forget the little things in life, but you never forget that first pain, that first love."

"Were you a fan of teenage tragedy songs, like 'Teen Angel' or 'Endless Sleep'?"

"I never really thought about *Teenage Angel of Death* in those terms when I recorded it. I'm sure, now, it looks like I wrote one big, long teen death song, but that was never my intention. I just wanted to tell the story of my unrequited love for Sarah Sue. That's what *Teenage Angel of Death* really is. It is a story of unrequited teenage love."

"And one heck of a story it is," Soda Jerk Perkins added, "Let me tell you, the listening audience. If you've never heard this out-of-print classic before, sit back and enjoy the Malt

Shop program in it's entirety tonight. But first, you're going to play a new cut you've added to the album."

"I thought it would be good to give an older and wiser interpretation of the songs I wrote back when I was a teenager."

"What's the first song you're going to sing called?"

"'Like It Was Yesterday.'"

"Ladies and gentlemen of the listening audience, sit back in your chairs and relax and enjoy the sounds of Buddy Brown."

From the Album

Buddy:
The mind is patchwork of yesterdays,
Blurring together as the memory decays.
One by one turning cloudy and gray,
And into the ether they soon blow away.

I wouldn't change how my life was written,
But there was another time when I was smitten,
With the girl from next door, my best friend,
And I thought I knew how my life would end.

But when I think of Sarah Sue Hayes,
All the years seem to fade into days.
Back when the future was a distant someday.
Ah, I remember it like it was yesterday.

I knew because God would answer my prayer,
To make Sarah Sue and Buddy the perfect pair.
That's how it would be if I was the author of my life,
I'd be the perfect husband, Sarah Sue'd be my wife.

But when I think of Sarah Sue Hayes,
All the years seem to fade into days.
Back when innocence was never betrayed,
Ah, I remember it like it was yesterday.

The mind is patchwork of yesterdays,
Blurring together as the memory decays.
One by one turning cloudy and gray,
And into the ether they soon blow away.

The Girl Next Door

From the Journal of Buddy Brown

This is so exciting. Mrs. Story has instructed her English students that the juniors of the class of 1957 must keep a diary over the course of the year to be turned in for *a grade*! Yeah! Of course, the boys were asked to keep a "journal" because diaries are for girls. I get to write for a grade. An "A" no doubt, but it's for a grade.

I've written stories my entire life. I make up stories all the time. I'd love to get them published in a pulp magazine, but I don't think my stories are quite good enough for publication. I'm sure I will send one out sooner or later, when I'm a much better writer. Sarah Sue loves my stories. She is the only person in the whole wide world that I share my stories with. My dad wouldn't understand and my mom would only say, "That's nice, dear." Oh, I'd be the laughing stock of the school if the kids knew I wrote "for fun".

And God-forbid anybody finds out I write song lyrics, even though I can't play the guitar very well at the moment.

Mrs. Story told us it wasn't hard to write a journal; you only had to write your thoughts. Don't edit yourself. They didn't have to be Pulitizer Prize winning novels or anything of the sort. They just had to be the thoughts we were having at the moment we were writing them. "Stream-of-consciousness" is what she called it. Just write what is in your head, you'll do fine, and you'll get an "A".

A-plus!

"Don't censor yourself," she advised us before moving onto the first required reading of the semester. I don't see what thoughts I would need to censor. I'm a good Catholic boy and I go to Confession once a week (okay, maybe once a month), but I never have anything to really confess. I don't think I do anything that can be categorized as a mortal sin. Venial sins. Sure. You can't escape those. Maybe coveting. Yeah, I guess I covet. I don't do it on purpose and it isn't like the object of my covetness has a boyfriend of any sort, but Jesus says that even thinking about a women in a sexual nature is coveting her. I guess in the old Biblical way of thinking, the object of my affections is owned by her father, so I am coveting another man's possession. But this is 1956 for pity's sake; we're half-way through the twentieth-century. Girls can make their own decisions on the subject of love.

It's a good thing this journal isn't going to be read by anybody (except for Mrs. Story), because I'd never live down the shame if the school found out I had a mad crush on Sarah Sue, literally the girl next door. Sure, we're best friends and all, since the age of four I might add, and we're always stuck to each other like glue, but they'd make fun of her *relentlessly* for being my girlfriend.

I can hear them now, "You're dating Mr. Brown? He's so gross; he eats his own boogers."

I'll never live this one down. I picked my nose once, in the third grade and nobody, and I mean nobody has let me forget that one. And why do the kids at the school call me "Mr. Brown"? It is baffling. I'm their age. I'm not an adult. I try to behave like an adult, always on my best behavior and such, but being called "Mr. Brown" is infuriating. I guess it could be worse. Brown is the color of so many gross things. Yeah. It could be worse.

Sarah Sue and I have been instant best friends since I moved into her neighborhood when I was four. My earliest memory isn't my birthday that year when nobody came to my birthday party expect Sarah Sue. It is one of those memories that seems like a memory because my parents have told the story so often I can almost see it in my head. I can see the kitchen and the cake with four candles on it. I can see Sarah Sue sitting next to me, helping me blow out the candles, because she is nice. She gave me bubbles which delighted me to no end, because it was so new. You can blow... bubbles? My mom loves to talk about Sarah and I "frolicking" around the back around blowing and popping countless bubbles until the bottle ran dry. How easily entertained we are as children. The events did happen, of course, but the memory I have isn't a real memory. But it should be.

My first "real" memory is rather embarrassing, but Mrs. Story, you are a grown-up and you also teach Health class, so you can handle it, I'm sure. Sarah Sue's older sister Stacy told her that boys were, how can I put this, "Different down there." So like lightning, Sarah Sue was over at my house insisting that I go into the bathroom with her. This struck me as odd, even at the age of five. You went into the bathroom alone. That was a private time to be alone with your thoughts and your bowel movement. This was time my father called "going to the library" with the sports page tucked under his arm or "going to see Ms. Jones", who I always assumed was the librarian. I carried on this tradition into my teenage years, but instead of the newspaper, I chose a monster magazine.

So, there we stood, in the bathroom, together. "Stacy says boys are different down there."

"Down where?" I asked and she responded by pointing at my zipper.

"There?" I asked also pointing at my zipper.

She nodded.

"Oh. Different how?" I just needed to know, but at the same time, I didn't really want to know.

"I don't know. She didn't say."

"We're different?" I asked.

"Yes. You show me yours and I promise I'll show you mine."

The foolishness of the moment was lost on a five year-old and I unzipped my trousers and pulled them down.

"What's that?" Sarah said, gasping and pointing her finger at it.

I can remember feeling flush if that is at all possible and embarrassed to no end. I pulled up my trousers, underwear, and zipper all in practically one motion.

"No, I want to see it," she said.

"No. I don't want you to see it again."

"I'll show you mine. I promised. You promised."

I was caught in the five year-old's quandary: "The Promise".

I pulled my pants back down and let her take a good long look. Sarah Sue looked at it with the same look that my mom makes when she is looking at meat in the butcher's shop.

She giggled. "It's so funny looking."

"It's normal," I said. "I'm normal."

"Okay, now I'll show my mine."

"No. I don't want to see yours."

"Why?"

"I don't know. What if it's gross."

"Your's was gross first."

"It's not gross."

"It was so gross. Now I want to show you mine."

"But I don't want to see what girls have."

"But a promise is a promise."

Crap. "The Promise". Twice in as many minutes.

Sarah hooked her fingers around the waist of her skirt and pulled it down. She stood there for a moment, a very long moment teasing me in her panties.

What could she possibly have? I had no idea. The imagination when allowed to run wild is such a terrible thing. Did she have two? What if it looked like a nose or some other body part?

Then she pulled her panties to the floor.

Nothing.

There was nothing there. I realize now after have taken anatomy class that were was a vagina there, but to a five year-old there was absolutely nothing there and I grew genuinely concerned.

"What happened to it? Were you in an accident?"

"I never had it. Whatever you have, I never had it. I'm a girl, you're a boy. You have what you have and I have what I have. I guess it fits."

Little did we realize that it actually does fit. Literally.

Sorry, Mrs. Story, but this is the stream of my consciousness.

From Sarah Sue's Diary

Dear Diary,

Buddy is so excited about this journal project, but I'm not so sure. He talked incessantly, while carrying my books as we walked home from school together, about how exciting it was to write down our own story. This is our story, the story of our life, and we get to tell it our way. And for a grade. I could only laugh.

I don't know if I could write my most private thoughts down in a diary. I've never kept a diary in my entire life. I'd be petrified if my mother found it or, Heaven-forbid, my father found it. I wouldn't be able to show my face at the dinner table if they knew what I actually thought. If they knew what actually went on in my head. A virginal Catholic girl simply doesn't have these kinds of thoughts.

I spent an hour tyring to find a place to hide this cursed notebook. I looked around my bedroom for a safe place to secret it away from prying eyes. I couldn't hide it in the bureau, my mom would find it putting away the laundry. Or under my mattress, what if she found it putting on fresh linens? The closet was also out of the question. There was no place to hide it anywhere.

Good, dear, honest Buddy, suggested that I give it to him to hide in his bedroom. His mother wasn't a snoop and his father respects a man's privacy because Buddy is a man now. His bedroom is like a bank that I will lock away my most personal belonging. My private thoughts.

I know in my heart that Buddy would never betray me by reading it. And with it safely out of the reach of my parents, I guess I'm ready to open up.

A little bit.

I don't know why I'm such a bad girl. I really don't. The Father would say I've got a wee-bit of the devil inside my soul. I just can't help it. I guess I'm not a really bad girl, but I'm not a good girl either. I don't do things bad girls do. I don't go to make-out point with boys or wear make-up. I dress nice. I act properly around everyone, except Buddy.

With Buddy, I can be myself. Which is a relief. Always acting like the good Catholic school girl that I should be is so very tiring. With Buddy, I can say what I want to say when I want to say it. I can do what I want and I very seldom embarrass Buddy.

Okay that's a lie. I embarrass him constantly and consistently, but he never holds it against me. He is my best friend and best friends let each other be themselves. That's what the best part of being best friends is.

I do know the day I let a wee-bit of the devil inside my soul. I know it to the day. It was the day of my first Communion.

Buddy was already an altar boy at Sacred Heart by the time I had my first Communion. He had already received his first Communion the year before and had his Sacrament of Reconciliation in order to be in a state of grace before receiving the Host. I can't remember why I didn't have my first Communion then, we are the same age after all.

Maybe my father objected to the entire Transubstantiation thing being a Methodist. He never let my mother forget that they would have been married "in sin" if he hadn't agreed to a Catholic ceremony, all because of her damned Catholic faith, because his "Goddamn" church wasn't good enough for the Pope, and if his faith wasn't enough for the Pope, well, "The Pope could just go..." I can't really write what he told the Pope to do to himself. It was both obscene and sacrilegious. Daddy also never forgave the Bishop for forcing him into a Catholic wedding ceremony and then forcing Catholic baptism onto all of his children. And he never forgave my mother for taking us to Mass each and every Sunday. He'd sit at the kitchen table, eating his breakfast while we readied ourselves in our Sunday Best, and he'd curse under his breath as we walked out the back door to go to Mass. I'm pretty sure this is why I finally had my first Communion, but first I needed to confess my sins to be in a state of grace with the Lord.

Buddy confessed his sins then and every Saturday since, but I have no idea what he has to confess. He is purer than the Pope. His conscience is stricter than Sister Mary Stick-up-her-butt. Saint Buddy, patron saint of...? What would he be the patron saint of? Heehee. Boys that play with themselves? Hell. He snacks his knuckles with a ruler over any bad thought or deed. Not in reality, but in his head. Always in his head that boy.

Anyway, I guess I got a taste of wine on my lips during the service, because I convinced Buddy to sneak into the rectory to steal a bottle of wine for us. Not the Holy Blood of Christ after it was Transubstantiated, oh, no, not even my little devil is that evil. Just a bottle of wine. It couldn't possibly be the Blood of Christ before it was consecrated on the altar. Could it? Didn't the priest just go down to the corner liquor store and buy himself some red wine like the rest of society? I didn't know and my little Jesuit friend Buddy didn't know either. So everything seemed Kosher. (Mixing religious metaphors won't make Mrs. Story proud.)

I'm sure it didn't take much to push either Buddy or myself to the tipping point with the wine. A few sips would have been all that was necessary to make us "think" we were drunk. We can both remember we acted the fool in the quiet dark of the rectory, the congregation having long left the sanctuary. We were wasted.

Poor Buddy began to panic about being drunk and worried himself until he was sick. Quite literally. He threw up in that special sink you use to put the consecrated wine down, so the Blood will return to the earth. I know girls aren't supposed to know about it, but Buddy tells me everything.

Buddy was distraught. He had received Communion not an hour before. He had thrown up the Lord. I could see him flipping through pages of the Catechism in his head, looking for the rules concerning vomiting the Body. There had to be some canon law about that, shouldn't there? I'm sure he wasn't the first and wouldn't be the last to puke up the Body of Jesus Christ our Lord and Saviour.

Mother always said the Father was a notorious drunk.

"Buddy, you puked in the special sink. Ashes to ashes and earth to earth, and so forth," I said trying to comfort him.

"Don't quote scripture to me at a time like this. I'm going to Hell. We stole communion wine and I puked up the Lord. If there is a reason for eternal damnation, this is it."

"It's not like the church has a coal-chute in the boiler-room that leads straight to the gates of Hell."

"Oh, Lord. I bet they do," he said, those wheels in his head beginning to spin out of control like a run-away train. "I know they do. I bet I've even seen it down there. I know I have. I have seen it! The priests aren't going to bury a sinner in consecrated ground. What do you think they do with bodies of the sinners? Straight done that coal-chute, straight to the Devil himself, and splash! into a cauldron of fire, I go! Oh, oh. I'm going to Hell for sure. And it's all your fault."

It's always my fault.

Little does Buddy know that it's me that is going to go to Hell. Straight down that coal-chute I will go.

From the Album

Buddy:

I met her on my birthday,
The year that we turned four.
I was new to the neighborhood,
She was the girl next door.

My mom invited the neighborhood,
But the sun was shining clear.
My "friends" played in their yards,
She was my only guest that year.

Friends forever, friends forever,
Nothing will tear us apart.
Friends forever, friends forever,
I'll own a little piece of her heart.

Sarah Sue:

There was a rainy day,
The year that we turned six.
I went over to play doctor,
He didn't even know he was sick.

"I promise to show you mine,
If you show me yours."
He blushed bright ruby red,
He'd never played doctor before.

Friends forever, friends forever,
Nothing will tear us apart.
Friends forever, friends forever,
I'll own a little piece of his heart.

Buddy:

Then on Easter Sunday,
The year that I turned seven.
I promised to be her friend,
Until the day I entered Heaven.

Her daddy wouldn't let her
Have any friends over to play.
I had a set of walkie-talkies,
And we'd talk night and day.

    Friends forever, friends forever,
    Nothing will tear us apart.
    Friends forever, friends forever,
    I'll own a little piece of her heart.

Sarah Sue:

After our first Eucharist
The year that we turned nine,
I made Buddy, good honest Buddy
Steal a bottle of Communion wine.

We got drunk for the first time,
On the blood of Emmanuel.
Buddy feared for our souls,
Said we'd both go straight to Hell.

    Friends forever, friends forever,
    Nothing will tear us apart.
    Friends forever, friends forever,

        We'll both go straight to Hell.

The Girl Next Door II

From the Journal of Buddy Brown

Mrs. Story made an assignment today that made me shudder to the bone. It think this might be the first assignment which I won't get an "A" on in my entire life. This is an assignment that I can't do. I just can't bring myself to do it.

She wants us to write a love poem in the style of Lord Byron or Percy Shelly. I'd rather be assigned to write the nightmare of Frankenstein than write a love poem. I've buried my feelings since I was fourteen; they lie festering in a cemetary of unrequited love. Can I dig up those feelings and inject them with the spark of life from the constant bolts of lightning to my soul I feel every time I see her? I can't let my Frankenstein's Monster, my love for Sarah Sue live. It would be an unholy creature. My Monster is an innocent soul, tepid and shy, a harm to no one but myself. I'm terrified if confronted by Sarah Sue, it may lash out in panic and fear and drive away the love of my life. The Monster will go tearing through the countryside with the peasantry armed with torches persuing me at every turn. How can she love a Monster like myself? If Sarah Sue ever found out... I shudder to think.

Anything in the world, except a love poem.

It's just that I cannot admit to anybody with the exception of myself that I am hopelessly in love with Sarah Sue, the girl next door.

I will write the assignment, of course. This is an impossibility. Buddy Brown not doing an assignment. Heaven-forbid. I just won't be in the style of Byron or Shelly. It'll be in the Negro-style of the Blues. I'm risking a "B" or even... an "F".

Oh, God.

I guess I'll sit at my Remington typewriter and wait for the devil to meet me in my bedroom so I can sell my soul to get a little of that wicked, wicked Blues.

```
                    Roses Are Blue


The Blues hurts so much,
What am I gonna do?
My Blues hurts so much,
What am I gonna do?
When you have no eartly idea
That I'm in love with you.


The love we could've had has died,
The Blues is very sad.
The love we could've had has died,
The Blues is so very sad.
In the cemetery is the grave
Of the love we'll never have.
```

I put roses on that gravestone,
Each and every day.
I put red roses on that gravestone,
Each and every day.
I mourn the words of love,
I'll never have the courage to say.

I asked the gravedigger if
He'd give that love back to me.
I asked the gravedigger,
"Can you give that love back to me."
He said to me, "Write her a letter,
Love'll live, you'll see."

Every day the mailman asks if
I've got letters to post.
Every day the mailman asks,
"You got letters to post?"
His bag is empty of the letter
I want to send the most.

Everyday the milkman asks if
My feelings have gone stale.
Everyday the milkman asks,
"Have your feelings gone stale?"
Today I told him, "No, sir,
But I can't post 'em in the mail.

Will I end up before a judge
For the crime of keeping silent?

```
Will I end up before the judge
For the crime of keeping silent?
I will live out the rest of my life
Living with this eternal torment.

The Blues hurts so much
'Cause roses are so blue.
My Blues hurts so much
'Cause roses are so blue.
When you have no earthly idea
That I'm in love with you.
```

Well, I got an "A" on my Blues poem. Mrs. Story asked if I was really into "race" music. She seemed genuinely concerned, maybe for my soul, I don't know. I told her that while most of the kids were into Rock 'n' Roll, I kind of liked Muddy Waters and other Blues from up in Chicago, that electrified, rockin 'n' rolling Blues; not that raw and eternally frightening Blues from Mississippi. There was something sinister about that Blues and being Buddy Brown, I certainly had cause to have the Blues.

She laughed.

A white boy with the Blues? She sent me back to my desk.

From Sarah Sue's Diary

Love is in the air,
I feel like such a square,
I was caught so unaware,
He is so, dear God, debonair.
If love is not for me, I'll despair.
Not having your heart, this I can't bare.

Of boys like you, I was told to beware.
For you my heart will I tear.
I will follow you, no matter where.
Can we have a steamy affair?
Will you with your blue eyes at me stare?
Our love will be so devil-may-care.
I have nary a care
In the whole wide world,
I'm such a lucky girl.
It fits me like a glove,
This thing we call love,
It's a gift from Heaven Above.

Dear Dairy,

   Why is it when you're in love, everything seems to rhyme?

I'm just a girl of sweet sixteen,
Not yet a woman or so it seems.
But I've met the boy of my dreams,
He's like an immortal James Dean,
With that pompador's sheen,
Streaked with hair fop cream.
Riding on that mean machine,
A bike fueled by gasoline.
He drinks straight kerosene.
His eyes sparkle, teeth gleam.
I'm the prettiest girl he's ever seen.

I'm so flustered I have to scream.

This was so unforeseen.

My first real kiss on Halloween,

Under the full moonbeam,

He's my king, I'm his queen.

Tells me his secret, his real name is Eugene.

He is so nice, not even a little mean.

About him, all day, I daydream.

I feel a little bit unclean.

My feelings are obscene.

His love will get me quarantined.

Of his love, I'll never be clean.

I'm so flustered I have to scream,

I feel like I'm going to blaspheme.

Johnny Angel, the boy of my dreams.

From the Album

Buddy: *One day after school,*
The year that I turned eleven,
I again promised to be her friend,
Until the day we entered Heaven.

She made me promise,
Promise to never, ever tell,
That her daddy beat her… no…
That down the stairs she fell.

Friends forever, friends forever,

> Nothing will tear us apart.
> Friends forever, friends forever,
> I'll own a little piece of her heart.

Sarah Sue: One day I missed school,
The year that we turned twelve,
Buddy saw my eyes bruised black,
"I was only hit by a loose shelve."

I cried on his shoulder until
My face was streaked red.
I couldn't tell Buddy, good honest Buddy
That I wished I was dead.

> Friends forever, friends forever,
> Nothing will tear us apart.
> Friends forever, friends forever,
> He'll own a little piece of my heart.

Buddy: On the happiest day of my life,
The year that I turned fourteen,
My best friend in all the world,
Became the prettiest girl I'd ever seen.

We'd been best forever friends,
We fit each over like a glove.
I knew that we be more than friends,
She was the girl that I would love.

Friends forever, friends forever,
Nothing will tear us apart.
Friends forever, friends forever,
We'll own a little piece of each other's heart.

Sarah Sue: On the happiest day of my life,
The year that I turned sixteen,
I saw Johnny Angel on his bike,
A bike fueled by gasoline.

I fell in love with him at first sight,
His leather jacket, his fenders of chrome.
I needed to tell my best friend the news,
So to Buddy, I rushed on home.

Friends forever, friends forever,
Nothing will tear us apart.
Friends forever, friends forever,

So to Buddy, I rushed on home.

SIDE A - SONG 4

Why Do Good Girls
Love Bad Boys?

From the Journal of Buddy Brown

Why is the man of her dreams, a nightmare for everyone else in her life?

I wish it was an actual nightmare, because if it was just a bad dream, an excruciatingly bad dream, then I'd be able to wake up from it. I'd wake up in the morning with the dawn's light streaming through my curtains and I'd know that Sarah Sue was mine and mine alone. That the nightmare of her being boyfriend and girlfriend with Johnny Angel would just be the worst kind of nightmare.

But every morning my father, coming home from the graveyard shift at the steel mill, wakes me up to get ready for school. "Hey, Champ," he'd say, "get up and at them. Hop in the shower, shave (little did he know I only have to shave once a week), and get ready for school." Then he walks across the hall into my parent's room and crawls into bed, exhausted. In an hour or so, once he was deep asleep, Mom will go in and quietly undress him.

Every morning since Sarah Sue dropped that Atom-bomb of a revelation that she and Johnny Angel were going steady, I pinch myself. I pinch myself really hard, until it smarts. But I know that this isn't a dream and that Johnny and my girl, I mean his girl, are together.

She could have any guy in school, anybody (well, not just anybody. Me.), but she chose the worst of the worst. Calling him a juvenile delinquent like Mrs. Story always does is a compliment. He is... Well, I assume profanity isn't allowed in this journal, so I will refrain saying what I want to say because I'll just have to confess it on Saturday.

The Father would call him the Anti-Christ. I call him my nemesis. Every good guy have to have an arch-nemesis. Batman has the Joker. Flash Gordon had Ming the Merciless. And I have Johnny Angel.

I wish that Sarah Sue could see Johnny through my eyes, her father's or Mrs. Story's eyes, or anybody with even a shred of common sense. I know that is a little insulting to my best friend. But love really is blind... and stupid.

Johnny Angel, with his hair fopped up with the perfect duck tail, cares about only one thing and that is himself and that stupid motorcycle. He makes Narcissus look like Casanova.

I don't pretend to be a prophet or a fortune teller who foresees the future (because I know that would be a sin worthy of the Pit), but this relationship will only end badly. I know that Sarah Sue will be crying on my shoulder when her heart is broken by this... miscreant. She will be destroyed while he has already moved on to sluttier pastures. A good girl is just too good for a bad boy. A bad boy needs a bad girl and in the end he will go back to his own kind and Sarah Sue will be left weeping. Tears staining my shoulder.

I will bite my tongue. Maybe that will smart enough to wake me from this living nightmare.

From Sarah Sue's Diary

Dear Diary,

This is an absolute dream. I hope I never, ever wake up. But every morning when I wake up, I'm so deathly afraid that this has all been a dream. I don't know what I would do if this was only a dream; to wake up and not be Johnny Angel's girl. That would be the worst, the absolute worst thing I can imagine. A nightmare!

So every morning, I run over to my jewelry box and pull down the mirror to reveal the secret little compartment in the lid and there I find his ring. My Johnny's special ring. He says, and he wouldn't lie to me, his little Sarah Sue, that it is a ring from a solider in the Roman legions. It is a little golden brass ring, tarnished quite bad and a little green in spots with a flat top. Sure does look like something ancient. Johnny won it in a poker game from some guy who fought the Italians in the war; the soldier-boy says he found it in the mud during the long days in the trenches.

Johnny smiled as he gave it to me. "I won that ring with the Dead Man's Hand, aces and eights. For what that's worth." His smile is as sharp as a switchblade. It cuts me deep every time I see it. Like when his fiery eyes give me an icy stare. Oh. The shivers tingle up my spine.

How I love this man.

If I ever wake up and find this was nothing but a dream, I'll have to kill myself.

From the Album

Unrequited Lovers: *Why do good girls,*
Oooooh wah, oooooh wah
  Love their bad boys?
Oooooh wah, oooooh wah
Oh, why, oh, why, do good girls,
  Love their bad boys?

Sarah Sue: *Is a bad boy's love worth the risk?*

His icy stares feel a little brisk,
My heart's love away it whisks.

Buddy: Why do good girls love bad boys?
Is the reason their fast toys?
Why do good girls love bad boys?
All despite the hearts they destroy!

Unrequited Lovers: Why do good girls,
Ooooh wah, oooooh wah
Love their bad boys?
Ooooh wah, oooooh wah
Oh, why, oh, why, do good girls,
Love their bad boys?

Sarah Sue: Did you see him ride me home?
Did you see his fender's chrome?
And his pompadour nicely combed?

Buddy: Why don't good girls ever see?
A bad boy's love can never be,
Why don't good girls ever see?
A bad boy's love ends in catastrophe!

Unrequited Lovers: Why do good girls,
Ooooh wah, oooooh wah
Love their bad boys?
Ooooh wah, oooooh wah
Oh, why, oh, why, do good girls,

Love their bad boys?

Sarah Sue:
He rides up in the dark of the night,
To defend my honor, he's willing to fight,
I know in my heart, he is my Mister Right.

Buddy:
Why do good girls play this game?
A bad boy's heart a good girl cannot tame.
Why do good girls play this game?
When the love ends, they'll never be the same.

Unrequited Lovers:
Why do good girls,
Oooooh wah, oooooh wah
Love their bad boys?
Oooooh wah, oooooh wah
Oh, why, oh, why, do good girls,
Love their bad boys?

Sarah Sue:
Why does my heart always skip a beat,
My love for him burns with enduring heat.
My love for him will his sins defeat.

Buddy:
Why is a good boy's love forever alone?
I wish I could commit a sin for which I could atone.
Why is a good boy's love forever alone?
I wish I had a bad boys heart for my very own.

Thank God!
Good Girls Love Bad Boys!

From the "Secret" Journal of Johnny Angel

I for the life of me can't understand how Mrs. Rottencrotch found out I wasn't writing this stupid diary. Sure she called it a journal, but it is a diary. You can call it what every you want to and it will still be a diary. And diaries are for chicks. She told me that I had to write in it each and every day and that I have to prove to her that I was actually writing. "How," I inquired in my good-little schoolboy voice, "if we do not have to turn them in until the end of the year, Misses Story?" I wish I could have wiped that grin off my face, because it would have saved me an hour in detention.

"You will show Buddy Brown what you have written every Friday before going home to the weekend. If you haven't written anything... substantial... you will spend Saturday in detention." SATURDAY detention?!? The nerve of that woman. The nerve of that woman to make her pet read my personal writings. Mr. Brown will not be allowed to read this diary if I have anything to say about it. Sure, it'll cost me a few hours in detention, but I'm not going to let some booger-eater read what I choose to write.

"Oh, and Eugene," God how I hate this woman, "I almost forgot. I don't want any profanity or greaser-slang in your journal. Keep that kind of language between you and your delinquent friends.

Well, ████, on me. You might as well chop off my ████ with a rusty butcher's knife. I'd like Mrs. Rottencroth to prove that those scratched out words are cuss words. PROVE IT!

I hate this school. I hate the goody-two shoes who walk the halls. I hate the jocks who think their better than me just because their athletes. Let's see them take me in a scrap. I dare them. I hate the preppy rich girls who flaunt their daddy's money in my face. I hate Mrs. Rottencrotch for being a stupid ████!

I can't believe that I got expelled from my old school and for what? Flushing a few, okay a dozen, Globe Salutes down the toilets in the girl's bathroom. How was I supposed to know that fireworks would actually blow the pipes to smithereens?

So I got expelled and sent to prissy Roncalli High. Now, it isn't a Catholic school, except that all the God-fearing brats from the Sacred Heart go to this school. Being around all these Catholics makes me worry for my soul.

Ha! That is if there was a God.

I do miss the Rebel Angels though. I don't get to mess around with them in class no more, but that may for the best. I shirley don't miss having detention with them every God-forsaken day. That is at least something... I don't know the words.

But they are here by the time school lets out for the day. They ditch their last class and make a bee-line across the tracks and up the hill to Roncalli to free me from my prison. When

I see my boys across the yard and my girl running to jump on my back of my hog. We ride away on thunder.

There is one thing nice about seeing a rich daddy's girl. I don't have to pay for squat. Gas from my tank. Food for my boys. I don't have to pay for do-diddy-squat. All my cash goes to playing cards or shooting dice.

Ace says I'm Sarah Sue's house Negro, but he got a serious butt-whooping for that crack.

The only problem with seeing a good Catholic school-girl is her virginity is locked tighter than the First National's vault. I don't mind getting to second-base almost every night, but just once I want to point to left field and score me a homer. Just once.

But that is why I have cheap cigarettes.

From the Album

Rebel Angels:
> *Thank God, good girls,*
> *Shooo wop, shooo wop,*
> > *Love their bad boys!*
> *Shooo wop, shooo wop,*
> *Good girls love their bad boys.*
> > *Thank the Lord!*

Johnny:
> *A Rebel Angels' love's worth the risk.*
> *Our icy stares feel a little brisk,*
> *Our love making is awfully frisk.*
>
> *So... why do good girls love bad boys?*
> *Is the reason our fast toys?*
> *Why do good girls love bad boys?*
> *Is it our motorcycle convoys?*

Rebel Angels: *Thank God, good girls,*
Shooo wop, shooo wop,
          Love their bad boys!
Shooo wop, shooo wop,
Good girls love their bad boys.
          Thank the Lord!

Johnny: *Nobody ever sees us drive them home.*
They'd stare at our fender's chrome.
Is my pompadour nicely combed?

Why do good girls squeal with glee?
Is it because our bikes wail like a bansee.
Why do good girls squeal with glee?
Is it because we offer no apology!

Rebel Angels: *Thank God, good girls,*
Shooo wop, shooo wop,
          Love their bad boys!
Shooo wop, shooo wop,
Good girls love their bad boys.
          Thank the Lord!

Johnny: *I ride up in the dark of the night,*
To defend her honor, I'm willing to fight,
She knows in her heart, I'm Mister Right.

Why do good girls play this game?
A bad boy's heart a good girl cannot tame.

> *Why do good girls play this game?*
> *When the love ends, they'll never be the same.*

Rebel Angels:
> *Thank God, good girls,*
> *Shooo wop, shooo wop,*
>> *Love their bad boys!*
> *Shoo wop, shooo wop,*
> *Good girls love their bad boys.*
>> *Thank the Lord!*

Johnny:
> *Why do their heart always skip a beat,*
> *Their love for us burns with enduring heat.*
> *We feel no shame when we cheat!*
>
> *Why do bad boys always get the girl?*
> *Our pompadour's got a nice little curl.*
> *Why do bad boys always get the girl?*
> *It's almost like we rule the world.*

SIDE A - SONG 6

Daddy's Angel

From Sarah Sue's Diary

Dear Diary,

I'm sorry Mrs. Story, but I can't... I can't write today. There can be no proof that this day ever happened. I've got to hide this cursed diary. I don't know where to hide it but I've got to find a place. Just in case. Just in case.

I can't write this, Buddy Brown. I know you would never break a promise... The Promise you gave me that you'd never read my diary. But I can't take the chance. I've written too much already.

Blessed Mary, please pray for me.

From the Album

Sarah Sue: *Dear Diary,*
              I'm my daddy's sweet little angel.
                    Daddy's Angel, Daddy's Angel
              Home's supposed to be like Heaven.
                    Daddy's Angel, Daddy's Angel
              Not living in the depths of Hell.

When my daddy's been a-drinking
I watch my every little, little word.
But he would still raise Holy Hell,
Over something he only half-heard.

He'd wrap his belt around his tight fist.
And beat me within an inch of my life.
My mama sat smoking a cigarette.
And played the good, faithful wife.

Dear Diary,
              I'm my daddy's sweet little angel.
                    Daddy's Angel, Daddy's Angel
              Home's supposed to be like Heaven.
                    Daddy's Angel, Daddy's Angel
              Not living in the depths of Hell.

My dear, dear sweet mama,
Doesn't even believe her own eyes.
She tells herself he's a good father,
She actually believes her own lies.

Sometimes he would hit me with his words.
I'd almost rather take the beating.
The emotional pain scars forever.
The physical pain is only fleeting.

Dear Diary,
    I'm my daddy's sweet little angel.
        Daddy's Angel, Daddy's Angel
    Home's supposed to be like Heaven.
        Daddy's Angel, Daddy's Angel
    Not living in the depths of Hell.
        Not living in the depths of Hell.

I'd lay tightly curled in my bed-sheets,
Trying to get to sleep in the dark of night.
But I couldn't catch a wink of sleep,
Always looking for that hallway light.

I'd cry myself to sleep every night,
Wondering why I deserved this fate.
I'd cry myself to sleep every night,
I love my daddy, I love my hate.

Dear Diary,
    I'm my daddy's sweet little angel.
        Daddy's Angel, Daddy's Angel
    Home's supposed to be like Heaven.
        Daddy's Angel, Daddy's Angel
    Not living in the depths of Hell.

Malt Shop Records

BUDDY BROWN & SARAH SUE
I WAS A TEENAGE ANGEL OF DEATH

SIDE B

1. THE WRONG SIDE OF THE TRACKS
2. CHEAP CIGARETTES
3. CHEAP CIGARETTES (Reprise)
4. TEAR STAINS ON MY SHOULDER
5. I NEED SOMEONE LIKE YOU
6. HEARTACHE HANGOVER
7. MORBID ANGEL

They say beauty is in the eye of the beholder.
Why won't our love's spark even smolder.
I love Sarah Sue with all my heart,
But this pain is tearing my soul apart.

I've fallen into a trap that all lonely boys fear.
She's crying on my shoulder, It's stained w/ her tears
I've fallen into a trap where I'm like her brother.
Why should I pursue my love? Why should I even bother?

    There are tear stains on my shoulder.
    All I have to do is, I have to do, is hold her.
    Yes, there are tear stains on my shoulder.
    All I have to do, I have to do is hold her,

She weeps and sobs over her lost love.
Little does she know we'd fit like a glove
I'd be both a best friend and a lover.
Her true feelings for me I wish she'd uncover.

She's cried on my shoulder since we were four.
I'd let her cry on my shoulder for a hundred more.
I will always be there for her in her time of need.
By being there for her, I'll plant love's growing seed!

    (Chorus)
All I need to win her heart is a little time.
I know you've heard this song and dance rhyme.
By being there for her, love's seed will grow.
Someone I'll be reprieved from love's death row.

There will come a day when she will open her eyes;
And love will come to her as a complete surprise.
She will look into my eyes and see that love must be.
She will love me with all her heart... voluntarily.

SIDE B - SONG 1

The Wrong Side
of the Tracks

From the Journal of Buddy Brown

Johnny Angel is stepping out of my Sarah Sue. I couldn't believe my eyes. I was ducking down the alley between the Woolworth's and the bank when I saw them. Johnny and some trollop named Annette making out on a stack of crates. The look in Johnny's eyes was the same look my pops gave me when I was seven and I walked in on him and my mom in a position the Father would consider sodomy. I didn't know at the time what my parents were doing at the time, but the image was burned into my brain like the picture on a television set down at the appliance store. The next look Johnny gave me, well that was I look I knew all too well. He was going to beat me up.

I never will understand why a girl like Sarah Sue Hayes would want to be with somebody like Johnny Angel. She is popular in school. She is on the cheer leading squad. She could, if she wanted to, date Chuck Miller, our All-American quarterback or be Senior class president next year. She can do anything she sets her mind to, but she lets her heart override her senses and she follows him around, well, like I follow her around.

But I knew I was about to get my lights punched out. You have to understand, Mrs. Story, that Johnny beats me up all the time. Not enough to leave a mark, but just enough that it smarts like the devil. He takes my lunch and any money I have so I can't buy a lunch. He makes me do his homework. And now after fearing a colossal beating, he was going to make me lie. Not the worst of offenses, you may be thinking, Mrs. Story, but this one is going to buy me a one-way ticket to Hell.

This is as close to betraying Sarah Sue as I will ever get if I'm lucky. I didn't care about the puppy-dog look Johnny gave me saying he would never hurt Sarah Sue, while wiping Annette's lipstick off his lips. That I should not hurt Sarah Sue by telling her that he was stepping out behind her back. That telling her would be worse than keeping this secret from her. The smooth-talking huckster had me convinced that I was doing Sarah a favor by keeping this between me, him, and this Annette chick.

I would also be in his debt. No more beatings. No more stolen lunches. No more fear. Nobody at school would ever mess with me again. He would have my back. In fact, he'd buy me booze if I so desired or cigarettes. He'd buy me some girly magazines, the European ones with actual intercourse. Or he'd buy my way into a poker game if I had urge to gamble.

Oh, and that if I told Sarah Sue, he'd kill me. Not beat the crap out of me, but kill me. He'd stick his switchblade into my belly and spill my guts all over my Chuck Taylors. I'd been threatened with death a hundred times before by bullies ever since kindergarten, but this was the first time I actually believed it.

From Sarah Sue's Diary

Oh, Diary!

I hate my father. I hate him so much. I don't care if I go straight to Hell for not honoring my father's wishes when it comes to Johnny, but I'm not going to let him talk about my boyfriend like that. It's... it's so infuriating for him to lay down ultimatums at me. I get good grades. I'm respectful. To tell me that I'm not allowed to see Johnny again. "Not allowed." I'm sixteen years old. I can make my own decisions. I am in love!

He thinks just because Johnny comes from the wrong side of the tracks that he is nothing but scum. Just because Johnny's father works at the steel mill shoveling slag day after day, doesn't mean he isn't making an honest living. Johnny doesn't have to go to law school or be a doctor to contribute to society, he can have a respectable job that provides for me and any children we may have.

But I shouldn't have called Johnny to come get me. I told him his motorcycle wouldn't do. No, his father's corvette wouldn't do either. He needed to come in his uncle's pick-up. I shouldn't have packed my bags, while my father screamed on the other side of the door, trying to knock it off its hinges.

I only hoped that Johnny would get there before the beating began. Daddy was going to give me the beating of my life when he saw my bag backed and ready to leave.

Why was I so surprised when he started pummeling my face with that leather belt wrapped tight around his fist. Why was I so surprised when I tasted blood and snot running over my lips. Why? I'd felt this kind of pain before. Dozens of times over the years in fact. I've tasted blood. I've tongued a missing tooth knocked down my throat. I've lied about falling down the stairs or walking into a door. The nurses at school are so ridiculously stupid and so gullible. They'd take my (and his) word for it every single time I came to school barely able to see, talk, or walk.

The beatings I could take. But the words. Oh, Blessed Mary, the words hurt even worse than his fists. The physical pain would heal in a day or a week, but the words, they have hurt for years. They still hurt. I have never healed from the words.

But after tonight, thanks to my sweet Johnny, he will hopefully won't ever touch me again. Probably not. Daddy will be even more angry with me after Johnny gave him a taste of what he has given me over these years.

I tried to smile seeing my father rolled up in a ball while Johnny punched and kicked him; hearing my father beg for his life, but the pain was so overwhelming. I couldn't even follow my Johnny as he ran from the house while my misguided mother screamed on the phone for the police.

I don't want Johnny going to jail for defending me. I know the law enough to know that Johnny might not go to jail if my father doesn't press charges. I just don't know what daddy will do in this situation. He may be too ashamed of his behavior to let it get around town that he beats his little girl. There have never been witnesses before. There has never been proof. But the police came to the house looking for Johnny, all because my mother called the police. The police saw me. They called for an ambulance to take me to the hospital. Dad tried to tell them that Johnny beat me too, but I refused to lie for my daddy this time. I couldn't lie against Johnny. Daddy might just let Johnny get away with this. This one time.

Now, I can only pray. It's all I've got at the moment. My faith in Jesus and my love for Johnny Angel.

From the "Secret" Journal of Johnny Angel

██████-ing-aye! I think I broke my hands. My knuckles are bleeding like a stuck-hog. I've been in a scrap or two in my day, but never have I beaten somebody to a bloody pulp like that. I think I may have killed a man tonight and that scares the ██████ out of me.

Stop shaking you sniveling weak little... Christ. Sorry. I shouldn't take the name of Sarah Sue's Lord in vain. I shouldn't. She wouldn't want that. I don't know if her dad still kicking or not. I got the Hell out of there as soon as he went limp. I don't even know if Sarah Sue is okay. ██████. I don't know. Why did I leave her there in that house? ██████!

But her mom, that stupid ▓▓▓ was on the phone with the cops. She was screaming into that phone that I was killing her husband. I couldn't be there when the cops showed up. A greaser just beat the tar out of a respected defense attorney.

Ha!

Respected?

Only a respectable man takes it out on his own daughter like that. People look down their nose at me because of my hog and my hair, but they smile and tip their hat to an abusive ▓▓▓ like that.

He stank of cheap booze. Bastard gets drunk and beats the ▓▓▓ out of my Sarah Sue. My dad is a world-class drunk and a boxer from his navy days. I've felt the sting of his belt and the bite of his buckle a lot, but once I got big enough to fight back, he never laid another hand on me. That I made sure of. But Sarah Sue, she can't fight back. She just too good a girl.

Why in the Hell am I writing this ▓▓▓ down? I don't know. I just feel the need to tell my story. Hell, that's it. I got to have a record of what happened tonight. The cops are going to come here any minute now. I just know it. ▓▓▓, I'm going to go away from a long, long time. I hope Sarah Sue will be waiting for me when I get out of jail. If I get out of jail. The bastard is probably dead. I'm just a loser from the wrong side of the tracks. They're going to fry my ▓▓▓ in the electric chair. The lights on death row are going to dim as the light in my eyes goes out.

I just lost it. My old man has lost it before. Maybe it runs in the family. But I never thought I'd ever loose control. You can't loose control during a scrap or you're going to get your butt handed to you.

I also never felt the desire to kill a man until tonight. To take pleasure in taking a man's life.

When I saw Sarah Sue cowering on the kitchen floor, her beautiful blue eye swollen shut and blood pouring out of her nose and that man standing over her with his fists clenched so tight his nails cut into his palms, I just snapped. It's one thing to treat a girl like dirt, but it's another thing entirely to lay your hands on one.

Not even my old man laid a hand on my mother. That was one rule he never broke. The worst beating I ever got in my life was when I was nine years old and I called my mother a bitch. (I'm not going to scratch that one out, Ms. Rottencrotch.) My dad stood up from in front of the radio and walked into the kitchen and beat me within an inch of my life.

"Never," he screamed at me, "never disrespect your mother. You can cuss out your old man, but you don't talk cross to your mother. She gave you life, you little ██████. Now apologize to your mother and get me a beer."

The thing is, officer (if you're the one reading this), I had to make sure he would never touch my Sarah Sue again. Even if that meant making Sarah Sue an orphan.

So this is what it feels like to kill a man.

Almost makes me want to pray for my ever-loving soul.

Almost.

I'm never going to see Sarah Sue again. She isn't going to be allowed to see me at the trial, except as a witness for the prosecution. The love of my life is going to send me away for the rest of my sorry life.

Maybe I just need to let her go. Let her love someone else. Somebody more worthy than a ████-up like me. If I lost control with her old man, maybe I could loose control with her. I couldn't live with myself if I hurt Sarah Sue, if I laid my hands on her. Maybe I just need to stay on my side of the tracks. Who needs that school when I'm going to end up in the steel mill or in the mines up in the mountains. A loser like me doesn't deserve such a great girl like Sarah Sue. I'm just going to hurt her in the long run.

Is this what they call a moment of clarity? I heard that somewhere. Probably Ms. Rottencrotch's class.

On the other hand, let some other jackoff get with Sarah Sue. Never.

From the Album

Buddy: *Johnny Angel rode into her life,*
He pierced my heart with a knife.
On a Harley-Dave gold and black,
He rode off with her on the back.

He was the toughest in and out of school,
He fought in bars and sharked at pool.
Grew up in those shotgun shacks,
On the wrong side of the tracks.

Unrequited Lovers: *Johnny Angel, Johnny Angel,*
The bad boy good girls adore.
Johnny Angel, Johnny Angel
Spat on his Chuck Taylors.

Buddy: *Sarah Sue could be Homecoming Queen.*
Johnny, well, he was just plain mean.
She could date the All Star quarterback.
He was from the wrong side of the tracks.

Sarah's daddy was a lawyer, always won,
Johnny Angel was a steel worker's son.
She was raised a good Catholic girl.
God didn't exist in Johnny's world.

Unrequited Lovers: *Johnny Angel, Johnny Angel,*
The bad boy good girls adore.
Johnny Angel, Johnny Angel

Why'd you walk up to her door.

Buddy: *"I forbid you to see that Johnny boy,"*
Her daddy said, more than a little annoyed.
"He might be a rapist or a maniac,
"He comes from the wrong side of the tracks."

Johnny Angel ran with a nasty bunch,
And every day, he stole my lunch.
If I tried to ditch him, he'd go berserk.
And every night, I did his homework.

Unrequited Lovers: *Johnny Angel, Johnny Angel,*
The bad boy good girls adore.
Buddy Brown, Buddy Brown,
Never'll get the girl he longs for.

Buddy: *Johnny Angel seemed to love Sarah Sue,*
How in the world could this possibly be true?
He was a better man for being with her,
But his wild ways, even she could not cure.

You see…
The only good I ever saw Johnny do,
Was when he rode up out of the blue,
And beat the tar out of her old man,
Who'd never again raise an angry hand.

Unrequited Lovers: *Johnny Angel, Johnny Angel,*

> The bad boy good girls adore.
> Buddy Brown, Buddy Brown,
> You would have given her more!

Buddy: I saw Johnny with a girl named Annette,
She was blonde to Sarah Sue's brunette.
Johnny said if I kept quite, he'd be in my debt.
But if I said anything, it'd be something I'd regret.

Johnny was stepping out on Sarah Sue,
I just didn't know what I could do.
If I said anything, Johnny would tear me apart.
If I said anything, it would break her heart.

Cheap Cigarettes

From the Journal of Buddy Brown

My Catechism teachers ever since kindergarten have warned about the dangers of selling one's soul to the Devil. I fear the Devil more than I fear God. I know this is blasphemy, but if I'm a good Catholic boy and I say my prayers at night, I shouldn't have to fear God. Should I?

I just never thought it would be so easy to buy my soul. It's the only thing I really have on this Earth and the Devil bought it as easily as I could buy a Baby Ruth at the Woolworth's.

I thought I knew what the Devil looked like. I've seen the monster movies during the Saturday matinee creature double-features. I know that the Devil is painted all-over with the same ghastly shade like hooker-red lipstick and with devilish horns, goat-legs, and a tail. Or he could, if he chose, look more like Vincent Price. This is the Devil they teach you about in Catechism.

But the Devil, my own personal Satan, looks exactly like Johnny Angel and he bought my soul with the spiritual equivalent of a book of grocery store trading stamps. Essentially worthless stamps that have the potential of greater rewards given time and patience. It didn't take cold hard cash or the promise of fame and fortune. I sold my soul to save Sarah Sue even the slightest amount of heartache.

I hope that my good deeds will award me with enough stamps to trade in for what I really, really want. The one item on the shelf behind the counter that tempts me everyday- Sarah Sue Hayes.

The problem is the Devil tricked me. He didn't give me the book of stamps so I could win Sarah Sue's heart, he took my book of stamps so I could never win her heart. All those good deeds, all those days of carrying her books while we walked home from school, all those nights where she cried on my shoulder over the things I wasn't supposed to know her dad did to her. I gave it all away to Satan himself. I thought I was helping Sarah Sue, but in the end, I was hurting her in the worst possible way.

The Devil leads you, ever so willingly, into betraying everything you hold most dear. This is, of all the reasons I know, why I'm going to Hell.

Annette is nothing more than cheap cigarettes. Johnny got a taste of her and now he's hooked, hopelessly addicted. That's exactly how cheap cigarettes work. I've sat in health class while they talked about how bad cigarettes are for you, that one day you might get lung cancer and die, yet Lucille Ball and Desi Arnaz hock Phillip Morris cigarettes during the opening of *I Love Lucy* every Monday night. Even as a teenager you knew the hypocrisy of how adults treat cigarettes. Everybody on television and in the movies smokes. My parents smoke. Everybody seemed to smoke, but nobody wants kids to smoke. Hypocrisy.

And Annette was the worst kind of cheap cigarette. More sawdust than tobacco. She is so easy on the eyes with a huge, I mean, huge bosom: bazooms as we boys like to call them. She paints her face like a hooker, or more actually, what I believe a hooker would look like with my overactive writer's imagination. I don't think I've ever seen a hooker before. I'm not even sure our town has hookers. Not that I'd know one if I saw one, but if I did see one, then they'd look exactly like Annette. As far as I know, Annette may be our town's county-fair award winning hooker. (Sorry, Mrs. Story, about the catachresis).

All I know is I have to keep Johnny's little habit a secret. Nobody can know that Johnny smokes his little cheap cigarettes. Except for one thing. He reeks of cheap cigarettes. The stench from her perfume, which she must buy by the gallon is all over his clothes. I've always wondered how kids who smoke keep the secret from their parents. They absolutely reek of cigarette smoke. Parents must be deaf, dumb, and dim. And as much as I hate to say it, Sarah Sue is too. How could she not know?

Annette flaunts it in her face. Okay, I'll admit they aren't exactly sucking face in the hallways, but it is pretty evident that they are mocking Sarah Sue. They are doing almost everything but sucking face in the hallways. It's like Johnny wants to get caught.

And then one day he was caught, red-handed in the girl's bathroom with his hand in the cookie jar (Okay, that's a major catachresis, but it's better than saying where his hands really where).

The jig was up and they started sucking face in the hallways.

Annette still whispers to me in Biology class that Sarah Sue had better watch herself. That if she tries to get Johnny back, there's going to be a cat fight. There was no way in Hell that a little "Miss-priss" like Sarah Sue would ever be with Johnny Angel again. The violence in her words scares me to my core and should scare Sarah Sue, but all Sarah Sue does is cry... on my shoulder.

From Sarah Sue's Diary

Dear Diary,

I never understood the term heartbreak. How could the heart actually break? Isn't it a muscle that continues to beat no matter what? How could the heart physically hurt from a stupid emotion? Well, I now know that this is just not true. The heart does break just like a crystal vase knocked off the mantle, shattering on the tile, raining glass into the fireplace. The shards of the glass that was my most fragile of hearts have torn into my chest, lacerating my innards. It hurts to breathe. I shudder to inhale. I shudder to exhale, fearing it will be my last.

Just when I think my tears have run dry, just when the red streaks staining my cheeks begin to fade, just when my nose stops sniveling, just when I think I can catch my breath, I think of Johnny Angel and my heartbreaks again. Tears flood from the dam of my heart, overflowing my eyes, and inundating the pastures of my cheeks.

You're being overly dramatic, Sarah.

If heartbreak has a taste, it is the taste of salt and snot. If heartbreak has a smell, it is the stench of his cologne lingering on your clothes. If heartache has a sound, it is the tenor of his voice echoing around your brain. If heartache has a image, it is the shade of his face staring at you when you close your eyes to sleep. If heartache has a feel, it is unbearable, excruciating, mind numbing pain.

I thought I had understood passion. The heat, the fire, the passion that I felt for Johnny Angel was what I believed to be the truest form of love. But as my Jesuit lawyer Buddy would remind me, passion in Greek means "suffering". Passion is one of those strange words that means one thing and the exact opposite in the same word. (Mrs. Story would appreciate my education poking through in moment of... I don't know.) Unbearable love and excruciating suffering.

Now, through a cloud of tears, I have seen a glimpse into the nature of God. "For God so loved the world that he gave His only Begotten Son..." The pain Jesus suffered during his Passion, his suffering on the cross was because God loved us so much. If God could feel this kind of pain because He loved us so much, why are we so shocked when it hurts so much when we love.

Love is the greatest gift we receive from God, from our parents, our friends, our lovers and if we lose that gift through death or loss, shouldn't it hurt? If we lose a grandparent to death or lose a precious keepsake, shouldn't it hurt?

Heehee.

I can't believe there is a smile on my lips, Mrs. Story, but I just remembered something that Mrs. Brown told me once when Buddy lost his most cherished childhood plaything. I don't understand why it has jumped from my memory to my consciousness, but I feel a little better just thinking about it. Care for a bit of a digression, Mrs. Story?

Buddy, poor honest Buddy, before he moved next door to me, when he was just a baby, this is so I don't know. I should be tearing my hair out or destroying every gift Johnny ever gave me and here I am telling a story about Buddy Brown as a baby. It just doesn't make any sense, Mrs. Story. This stream-of-consciousness writing is the strangest thing I have ever encountered. I want to weep, to wail, to cry until I die from the pain, but I need a laugh. So here it is.

Most babies have a cherished toy- a stuffed bear, a rag doll, or a blankie, but Buddy as a baby had a titty-rag.

"What exactly is a titty-rag?"

I'm glad you asked, Mrs. Story.

A titty-rag is nothing more than a cotton-diaper that apparently a baby Buddy was quite fond of. He slept with it and carried it everywhere he toddled to. You wouldn't find Buddy without his most beloved titty-rag.

"Why did the Brown's call it a titty-rag," you ask?

I'm glad you asked.

Whenever Buddy wanted a titty, (i.e. needed to breast-feed) and Mrs. Brown didn't have the time or the patience, they gave him his titty-rag to pacify him.

So when he wanted a titty, they gave him his rag.

Then one day, when they were moving to our little town, three-year-old Buddy was waving his titty-rag in the wind out of the cracked window in the back seat of the car, and whiz, it flew out of his hands, lost forever along some remote stretch of highway. He cried and cried because he lost his titty-rag. He begged them to stop the car and go back for his titty-rag. The Browns did not want to stop on some strange highway and look for a stupid cotton-diaper. So they let him cry himself to sleep in the backseat of the car.

Now, Mrs. Story, my little devil needs to add a little something to this story: I always thought that someday when Buddy Brown is married to some fine woman and has a couple of children and he feels a little, well, randy, and wants her titty and his wife isn't in the most passionate of moods, all she has to do his give him one of the baby's clean cotton-diapers, and he would be, as he was a child, pacified.

Heeheehee.

Buddy, even when he isn't in the same room with me, finds a way to make me feel better. Even as a ghost, Buddy can always make me smile, make me laugh. He's always there for me, will always be there for me. My best-friend. My only friend. My only true friend. I need to thank God that He moved the Browns next door to my family all those many years ago. I don't know what my life would be like if good honest Buddy didn't live right next door. I can't imagine how my childhood would have played out if he wasn't the nicest, kindest, sweetest boy in the world. He has never tried to pick a fight or talk down to me or be cruel to me for no reason.

Don't get me wrong, he's not perfect. He has his own personal demons, however insignificant imps that they are, he is not perfect. He worries so much it can be a distraction, a cause of irritation. Always so worried he has offended me with an off remark; asking me if we're still "okay". We'll always be okay. We'll be friends until the end of time. He's also kind of bull-headed when he sets his mind to something or believes something. Like evolution. No matter how much he believes in God and fears damnation in the pit, that brilliant mind of his is always searching for answers. Answers to math or history questions, answers to the mysteries of the universe. Why are we here? How did we get here? Are we the children of monkeys? Why can't he just accept what the priest teaches and believe God is the Creator of all? Sometimes there is no getting through his thick skull. Here I am trying so hard to knock Buddy down a peg or two, but his friendship, no matter how pure and honest it is, can be so smothering sometimes.

Don't be so hard on your best-friend, Sarah Sue. He is your best-friend, remember that always and cherish it. He has such a good shoulder to cry on.

I do look forward to meeting his future wife. I'll stand with the congregation of the Sacred Heart as my sweet, honest Buddy prepares to vow to be her's for better, for worse, in sickness, and in health, in good times and in bad, in joy as well as sorrow, to love and to cherish her; from that day forward unto death do they part. And he is actually going to mean every Blessed word and keep them in his heart until the day he dies. She is going to be the luckiest woman in the world.

Just like when Buddy cried himself to sleep over his precious titty-rag, I've cried myself out.

Good-night, Diary. The night doesn't appear so pitch black anymore and the morning looms a little brighter.

From the Album

Buddy: *Sarah Sue…*
How can I tell you' bout a woman,
That you've never met.
So, before you do something,
That you might just regret.
Johnny says she may not look like,
She could pose much of a threat.

Johnny says…
She's going to smoke you,
Just like a cheap cigarette.

She's going to smoke you,
Just like a cheap cigarette.

Sarah Sue…
I know you love your Johnny,
'N his daddy's smokin' hot corvette.
But that woman will teach you some tricks,
That you haven't even learnt yet.
She'll make you break out,
Into an ice cold sweat.

Johnny says…
She's going to smoke you,
Just like a cheap cigarette.
She's going to smoke you,
Just like a cheap cigarette.

Sarah Sue: *Good honest Buddy,*
I won't get too riled,
Or get myself all too upset.
You haven't heard it all,
You haven't finished your story yet.
I'm a good honest women,
This I won't soon regret.

I'm sure Johnny says…
She's going to smoke me,
Just like a cheap cigarette.
She's going to smoke me,

Just like a cheap cigarette.

Good honest, Buddy…
If I pick a fight over him,
It'll be a day that I'll regret.
If I mess with this other girl,
I may never see another sunset.
I won't ever play a game…
A game of Russian-roulette.

Johnny may say…
She's going to smoke me,
Just like a cheap cigarette.
She's going to smoke me,
Just like a cheap cigarette.

Buddy Brown,
I know I'll always love him,
But now I've lost this bet.
I've never, ever get over him,
But I have no… no regrets.
But I'm going to promise you,
I won't mess with Cheap Cigarettes.

SIDE B - SONG 3

Cheap Cigarettes (Reprise)

From the "Secret" Journal of Johnny Angel

I can't tell you how much fun Cheap Cigarettes is. That is my playful little pet name for Annette. The name Annette reminds me too much like that hot chick from that little kiddie show, *The Mickey Mouse Club*. I just can't look at my smoking hot Annette and call her Annette. Who wants to make-out with their sexy girl and think about some chick with Mickey Mouse ears on? So I figured "cheap cigarettes" rhymes with "smoking hot Annette". Who says an delinquent can't be romantic with poetry, huh, Ms. Rottencrotch?

With Cheap Cigarettes, I'm the Great Bambino of Love!

From the Album

Johnny:　　　　*Gotta tell you 'bout a woman,*

That you've never met.
Before you do something,
That you're gonna regret.
She may not look like,
She could pose of threat.

Rebel Angels: *She's gonna smoke you,*
Just like a cheap cigarette.
She's gonna smoke you,
Just like a cheap cigarette.

Johnny: *She's like no other woman,*
That you've ever met.
She'll teach you some tricks,
You haven't learnt yet.
She'll make you break,
Into an ice cold sweat.

Rebel Angels: *She's gonna smoke you,*
Just like a cheap cigarette.
She's gonna smoke you,
Just like a cheap cigarette.

Johnny: *Now don't get riled,*
And get yourself all upset.
You haven't heard it all,
I ain't finished my story yet.
You're a woman, Sarah Sue,
I'd just like to forget.

Rebel Angels:

She's gonna smoke you,
Just like a cheap cigarette.
She's gonna smoke you,
Just like a cheap cigarette.

Johnny:

I know you love me,
But you've lost this bet.
You'll never get over me,
But I have no regrets.
Why don't you play…
A game of Russian-roulette?

Rebel Angels:

She's gonna smoke you,
Just like a cheap cigarette.
She's gonna smoke you,
Just like a cheap cigarette.

Johnny:

If you pick a fight over me,
It'll be a day that you'll regret.
If you mess with this girl,
You'll never see another sunset.
I promise you, Sarah Sue,
Don't mess with Cheap Cigarettes.

Rebel Angels:

She's gonna smoke you,
Just like a cheap cigarette.
She's gonna smoke you,
Just like a cheap cigarette.

Tear Stains On My Shoulder

From the Journal of Buddy Brown

Sarah Sue never had to sneak into my house. When she wanted to visit me, all she had to do was walk up the stoop, ring the door bell, and my mother would simply say, "He's in his room," Sarah Sue would stroll down the hallway to my room and she would simply close the door behind her. My parents never had to worry about any hanky-panky going on in my room. I'm sure that a little part of them hoped there would be some hanky-panky going on. My dad was a man and knew what teenage boys had going on in their head. He had never forgotten what thoughts went through his mind as a teenager, even when the Depression was raging; not even the Depression can dull a teenage boy's urges. It fact, it probably fueled them.

My mother, my dear, sweet Catholic mother secretly hoped that her son would have a little hanky-panky with Sarah Sue. She had told me how much Sarah Sue was like a daughter to her, and if I knew what was good for me, I'd make Sarah Sue her daughter, bring her into our family through the bounds of Holy Matrimony, and give her my father's name. That is one thing about Catholic mothers, okay there are two things about Catholic mothers, guilt-trips and blatant nudging. There was no denying my mother wanted me to marry Sarah Sue. There was a part of me that wished we lived a hundred years ago when there were arranged marriages. That would solve so many of my problems. If my father and her father agreed to let their children marry, I'd be with Sarah Sue for the rest of our lives. It could be so simple.

But we live in the progressive 1950's where girls want a knight-in-shining armor to sweep them off her feet. I'm no knight. I'm not even a page or a serf. I'm the court jester. No princess wants to marry the court jester. No, wait. I'm not the court jester. I'm a eunuch. An impotent eunuch any Sultan would trust with the hundreds of wives in his harem. There is no danger that I would violate his harem. Poor, impotent Buddy Brown. So impotent my parents allowed me, a red-blooded American teenager, to have a girl alone in my room.

With. The. Door. Closed.

There she was, in the privacy of my room, the privacy my parents afforded me as a young man. She laid with me on my bed with her head resting on my shoulder as if I were a soft pillow. She cried so softly.

If some Peeping Tom looked in my room at the moment, he would think we were young lovers. But we weren't. We were the farthest thing from young lovers. I loved her in that moment. I wanted to kiss her. I wanted to caress her. I wanted to violate the trust my parents put in me by quietly making love to her. But I couldn't. I wanted to profess my love to her, my undying, unconditional love for Sarah Sue. But I couldn't.

I wanted to see the spark in her eye. The look I've seen girls give their boyfriends; the look I've seen Sarah Sue give Johnny Angel. It is a look that I want a girl to give me when we stare into each other's eyes.

The constant desire to express my undying love for Sarah Sue is tearing my soul apart. The pain is unbearable to know, to know in the deepest recesses of your heart, that she will not reciprocate that love. I've fallen into that trap all lonely boys fear. The girl I love more than life itself is crying on my shoulder over the pain inflicted on her by another man.

If I was the man she wanted me to be, I'd kick the snot out of Johnny Angel for hurting my Sarah Sue. But I'm not that kind of man. I'm the kind of poor, sad loser to believes that he can win the heart of his affections simply by loving her, by letting her cry on your shoulder until it is stained with her tears.

I've fallen into a tiger trap that I cannot escape. Why should I even bother any more?

Because you know you'll be there for her. That's why.

You were there for her when your were both six and her cat was hit by a car and she needed a shoulder to cry on. You were there for her when the bank almost repossessed her father's house, and she thought they'd have to move away and she needed a shoulder to cry on. You were there for her when her grandmother died and she needed a shoulder to cry on. You were there for her when her father beat her and she needed a shoulder to cry on. You will be there someday if her husband leaves her for another woman or if she loses a child in miscarriage or just about any kind of pain that is inflicted on her over the course of her life and she needs a shoulder to cry on.

You'll always be there for her.

I just have to be patient; I need to have the patience of a Saint. If I'm there every time she needs me, she will finally see. One day she will look into my eyes and see the love that just has to be. She will love me with all of her heart voluntarily.

She will speak those words I long to hear, "I love you."

From the Album

Buddy: *They say beauty is in the eye of the beholder.*
Why won't our love's spark even smolder.
I love Sarah Sue with all of my heart.
But this pain is tearing my soul apart.

I've fallen into a trap that all lonely boys fear,
She's crying on my shoulder, it's stained with tears.
I've fallen into a trap where I am like her brother.
Why should I pursue my love? Why should I even bother.

There are tear stains on my shoulder.
All I have to do— I have to do— is hold her.
Yes, there are tear stains on my shoulder.
All I have to do— I have to do— is hold her.

She weeps and sops over her lost love,
Little does she know we'd fit like a glove.
I'd be both a best friend and a lover.
Her true feelings for me I wish she'd uncover.

She has cried on my shoulder since we were four.
I'll let her cry on my shoulder for a hundred more.
I will always be there for her in her time of need.
By being there for her, I'll plant love's growing seed.

There are tear stains on my shoulder.
All I have to do— I have to do— is hold her.
Yes, there are tear stains on my shoulder.
All I have to do— I have to do— is hold her.

All I need to win her heart is a little time.
I know you've heard this song and dance rhyme.
By being there for her, love's seed will grow.
Someday I'll be reprieved from love's death row.

There will come a day when she will open her eyes.
And love will come to her as a complete surprise.
She will look into my eyes and see that love that must be.
She will love me with all of her heart… voluntarily.

I Need Someone Like You

From the Journal of Buddy Brown

As I combed her hair with my fingers, as she softly wept with her head on my chest, the words were slowly forming by my tongue. Tears welled up in my eyes as my breath began to push the three immortal words past my lips, when I heard her, through her snobs say, "Buddy Brown, I need someone like you."

I caught my breath and inhaled the words of love I was almost prepared to speak. Those immortal words I desired to hear her speak were about to be uttered by her soft, poutful lips. I shuddered as quietly as I could. Could Sarah Sue be about to profess her love for me? I didn't know. I couldn't know.

"I love you," she finally said. Those three simple words I dreamed of hearing since I was four years old. She actually said them. My soul soared to heights of Heaven to sing with the angels, "She loves me" and dove into the depths to Hell to mock the devils with "She loves me!" She had actually said, "I love you," but I knew that there was more she wanted to say when she drew a long breath. "Like the brother I never had.

"Oh, Buddy, why can't I meet someone like you. Someone like you, *but not you.*"

I died a little inside when I heard those ill-fated, poorly chosen words. This is not true. I died a lot inside. If God the Father was a wise and benevolent God, he would have given me a heart-attack in that moment so I could have died peacefully with my beloved Sarah Sue in my arms. Instead, I had to suffer the agony of heart-ache while Sarah Sue still wept ever so softly, her tears staining my shoulder again.

"Why aren't more boys just like you," she said so softly, so sweetly. "You are so nice, so kind, so caring. You know how to treat a girl right and you have no desire to pick fights. You wouldn't look at other girls if I were your girlfriend."

"If you were my girlfriend?" I implored. "Why couldn't you be my girlfriend? Why couldn't I be your boyfriend?"

She sat up on her elbow and looked at me in the eye and there was no spark. She didn't look at me like that. She looked at me like she had just caught me raping her cat. She looked horrified for a split-second before her look turned to one that was even worse... pity.

"Because you don't make my heart flutter."

"I could. I would," I said, choking on the words.

She put a finger on my lips, then said, "Our love is the kind of love that survives the test of time. We will love each other until the day one of us dies, and even beyond that I am sure. But our love is not the love that you fall into. A girl wants to fall desperately, passionately to fall in love with a boy. This is not the kind of love I have for you."

"And if I want that kind of love," I said before my senses had a chance to stop me. If we were going to have this argument, then we were going to have this argument, our friendship be damned. "I want that kind of love from you. I want to give that kind of love to you. You know I do. You have known since the day we first met that I. Love. You."

"I can't give you the kind of love you are asking for. That love wouldn't be real."

"Real? What is real? We have been best friends since we were children. We have shared every single moment of our lives. We have celebrated the good times together and mourned together when there were bad times. We love each other more deeply than any other love possible."

"But its not a romantic love, a passionate love, Buddy. Can't you understand that I'll always love you as a friend. I'll always need you as a friend; count on you to be there for me as a friend until the day that I die. I know this is the love that you will give me. The kind of love you need to give me."

"But... but I love you. I want to go steady with you. I want to give you my class ring. I want all of Roncalli to know that you are my girl. I'll go into my mother's room, get my grandmother's wedding ring and propose to you this very minute. If it's something you want, I'd do anything for you."

"Then, Buddy, don't."

"Don't what?"

"Just don't."

She turned away from me and sat on the edge of my bed crying. As much as Johnny Angel had broken her heart, I think, no, I know, she realized she had just broken my heart. That she hurt me as nobody else could.

Sarah Sue knew pain like nobody else I know. Her father beat her with his belt and scarred her his words. Johnny could be cruel to her, too. Johnny could cheat on her with Cheap Cigarettes and she'd just swallow the pain. Now, I could see it in her tear-blurred eyes as she peaked over her shoulder at me, that she realized that she hurt me not with cruelty but with her love- the kind of love she did have for me.

I have no doubt Sarah Sue thought she gave me a compliment she when she said those painful words, "Why can't I meet someone like you. Someone like you, **but not you.**" It was, however, the cruelest thing anybody has ever said to me during my short life.

She could have said "I want some Doppelgänger of you; some phantasmic Doppelgänger who looks like you, talks like you, treats me exactly like you treat me, loves me as you love me, but not actually you. No, I couldn't love you, but let Vincent Price strap you to a table in his laboratory, stick an impossibly long needle in your heart, and steal every sweet, kind, and loving quality you have and inject it into someone else, then I could love that unnatural creature. But love you? Don't. Make. Me. Laugh!"

I don't really know how long we sat crying in silence, before she got up the courage to leave my bedroom. We didn't speak again the next day (edit: or for a very long time). I never in my most fearful nightmares thought our friendship would end because we both loved each other too much. We had loved each other so deeply, just differently. But because of this knowledge, the love we did have for each other died and I buried it in the cemetery of unrequited love.

From the Album

Sarah Sue: *I love you like you're my brother.*
As I friend I'd never have no other.
You just don't make my heart flutter.
I need someone who is…

Our love is forever, 'till our lives are through.
Our love's not the love that you fall into.
That love I won't ever be sharing with you.
I want someone who is…

            Someone like you- but not you – just
            Someone like you- but not you.

Our love wouldn't be real, that I can't pretend.
I'll always, always count you a friend,

Until the world comes to a bitter end.
I want someone who is...

I love you in a special way, Buddy Brown.
You're always there when the sun goes down.
You're a great friend who will always be around.
I want some one who is...

> Someone like you- but not you – just
> Someone like you- but not you.

I need someone who will always be true.
I need someone who is never really blue.
I need someone who binds my soul with glue.
I need someone who is...

My lover has to be my best friend,
So our love will never come to an end.
I can't stand the pain of my heart's rend.
I need someone who is...

> Someone like you- but not you – just
> Someone like you- but not you.

I need a lover who is a friend like you,
I need a lover who'll do things a little taboo.
I need a lover who I can have a steamy rendezvous.
I need someone who is...

I want someone who'll stay out after curfew.
I want someone who'll get a tattoo.
I want someone who's got a little voodoo.
(But at the end of the day)
I want someone who is...

      Someone like you- but not you – just
      Someone like you- but not you.

Heartache Hangover

From the Journal of Buddy Brown

I don't know what a hangover feels like. I don't think I've ever actually been drunk. I know what alcohol tastes like: Communion wine tastes like wine, my dad slips me a beer every now and again while we listen to the baseball game (never a whole beer, just enough sips to get a taste, which is, thankfully, just one), and I've snuck a glass of cooking sherry once, which is just awful- almost as bad as baking chocolate. It might be labeled one thing but it's something completely different and will ruin your day.

So if I've never drank enough to get drunk then I've never drank enough to get a hangover. Which I'm thankful for. I've seen my dad hung over before. It's not pretty. The headache is one thing, my mom's relentless I-told-you-so's are an entirely different world of hurt.

But today, the morning after I professed my love for Sarah Sue; the morning after she told me she wanted someone like me, but not me, the night our friendship ended, I'm feeling so completely hung over. My eyes hurt from crying so much. My nose feels like its going to fall off after blowing my it so much from my weeping and sniveling. And my heart just aches. It hurts so much, I want to rip it from my chest like some voodoo priestess and sacrifice it on the altar of some heathen gods. This thing called "love" is the worst kind of addiction.

What I am feeling this morning before school is what I want to call a "Heartache Hangover". I loved and lost and am therefore Heartache Hung over. I had a feeling of supreme intoxication when I heard Sarah Sue say "I love you" and for that moment, however brief, I thought she meant it, but now I am paying the price for that feeling of euphoria. I should never have combed my fingers through her hair. I should never have drank in her scent while her head rested so gently on my chest. I should never have let those words pass my lips.

If you don't drink, you don't get drunk, and therefore you won't get hung over. If you don't love, you won't feel loved, and therefore you won't get heartache hung over.

I've heard the cure for a hangover is just to get drunk again, but I don't have anybody to love. There is no other girl in my life other than Sarah Sue. Was in my life, I mean. I don't have any Cheap Cigarettes to smoke. Maybe if I drowned myself in drink, maybe I wouldn't be heartache hung over, I'd just be good old-fashioned hung over. My parents have never lock the liquor cabinet because they know their son would never drink their booze. I could see the cabinet from the kitchen where I sat eating my flapjacks, eggs, and three thick strips of Kosher bacon (I know there isn't any Kosher bacon, Mrs. Story, but it makes the Catholic in me chuckle).

I wondered what whiskey tasted like. My parents told me they used whiskey to sooth my gums when I was teething, but I was just a baby. Who'd remember that? I wondered if drunkenness would dull the pain. I wondered if a real hangover was preferable to the feeling I was having. Now I know why my mother calls alcohol a demon. Right now, it is so tempting.

I was so heartache hung over when I got to school that morning, walking there for the first time without Sarah Sue and carrying only my own books, that I didn't notice Johnny

Angel had returned to school and Annette was no where to be seen. I didn't hear the giggling of the girls as I walked down the hallway. If I had, I'm afraid I would have thought they were laughing at me because I was in love with Sarah Sue or worse, torturing Sarah Sue because Mr. Brown was in love with her. I was so oblivious to the world around me that as I walked home from school, having not remembered a blessed thing I was taught that day, having failed every test I took (a first), that I didn't even see Sarah Sue get on the back of Johnny Angel's motorcycle and ride off with the wind in her brunette hair.

I'd like to think I didn't notice all of these things, but this is a lie. I have lied to you, Mrs. Story. I have lied in my journal. I have lied to myself. I saw and heard it all.

This was the worst day of my life. It was day of such bleak misery John Steinbeck would be proud of me for chronicling it in my own personal *Grapes of Wrath*, this dustbowl of my own making. There is no hope anymore. When I look at the world around me, it looks as grey as a television set in the window of Greenbergs. Sadness whips around my head like a dust storm. Unlike Tom Joad, there is no hope for me in California or anywhere. My love will whither and die here and just blow away.

I wish suicide was not a mortal sin, that my soul wouldn't be damned in the Pit for all Eternity, because all day I was trying so desperately to figure out in my head how to tie a noose.

All because of a Heartache Hangover.

From the Album

Buddy:
I'll never be loved by my best friend,
I wish my life would come to an end.
I'm as lucky as a three-leaf clover.
I've got a bit of a heartache hangover.

My heart hurts so bad, I can hardly think.
I can't bring myself to drown in drink.

I wish I could wish my troubles away.
My friendship with her, I can't betray.

Johnny Angel came riding back,
From the wrong side of the tracks.
Johnny laid it on thick like a fog.
I felt like a wounded old hound dog.

(Music comes to a end.)

You might think this song's over.
I'm a bit heartache hung over.
I'm as lucky as a three-leaf clover.
I've got a bit of a heartache hangover.

(Music resumes.)

I have always stood beside Sarah Sue,
He'll just leave her heart black and blue,
But Sarah Sue believed all of his lies.
She went back to him, I can't believe my eyes.

Johnny say's that he'll never again act mean,
That she'll be his own little Prom Queen.
He'll take her to the Stairway to Heaven Hop.
That he'll cut his hair down at the barbershop.

This is the part of the song, I can't bring...
I just... I just can't... bring myself to sing.
Johnny tells me he'll give her anything.
He's going to surprise her with an... I can't bring myself to sing.

(Music comes to a end.)

You might think this song's over.
I'm a bit heartache hung over.
I'm as lucky as a three-leaf clover.
I've got a bit of a heartache hangover.

From the "Secret" Journal of Johnny Angel

Hey, Missus Story, have I got the greatest news in the world. I got my girl back again. Sure, I screwed up royally, but you'll be glad to know that I have learned my lesson. I have given up Cheap Cigarettes. I am going to walk the straight and narrow now. I have seen the light. No, I haven't found Jesus or nothing foolish like that, but I know now what a man's responsibilities are. If you're going to be in a grown-up relationship with grown-up responsibilities, you just have to act a certain way. The Rebel Angels won't understand that I've got to step up to the plate, not to get to third base or even hit a home-run. I'm sorry if the sexual metaphor is lost on you, Missus Story. Metaphor? You actually taught me something, you crazy old broad. I've got to step up to the plate and be a man. Not the kind of man my father is or even the kind of man Sarah Sue's father is. I've got to be the kind of man, I hate to say it, that Mr. Brown is.

Who is Mr. Brown, you ask? Don't ask, because I won't tell you. It's so embarrassing.

I saw the streamers and posters for prom, the Stairway to Heaven Hop (such a stupid name), and since the dance is coming up so soon, so I'm going to get me a tux and take Sarah Sue to the prom. If your chaperoning it, Missus Story, you like all the girls in school, will be shocked to their knee socks when I walk into the gym with my hair cut. Not like a Marine or anything so radical, but a haircut I'd like to think you would like.

While I don't think since Sarah Sue is a junior, she will be crowned Prom Queen, but I'm going to tell you a secret, Missus Story. Sarah Sue will have not to wear that piece of crap tin crown to be the Prom Queen. She's going to feel like a real Queen, because I'm going to give her a real diamond ring. I'm going to get down on one knee in the middle of that stinking gym, in front of all these people I cannot stand, and I'm going get down on one knee and propose to my Sarah Sue. She's going to be the future Mrs. Eugene Clark.

Yes, Johnny Angel dies at the Stairway to Heaven Hop.

SIDE B - SONG 7

Morbid Angel

From the Journal of Buddy Brown

I have decided that suicide is a mortal sin and I want the eternal rewards of Heaven. But like a Jesuit lawyer, I have found a loop-hole to the different ways to enter Heaven. You can't take your own life, but you can most certainly put yourself in situations that will get you killed. My suicidal tendencies lasted all of a dark and gloomy day, but now that I know I can die any number of other ways, I am so much happier. If I can sneak past St. Peter and slip through the Pearly Gates, I'll take it.

My fantasies have turned to the morbid. In the past, when I thought of the ways that I would win the heart of my Sarah Sue it usually involved a dozen red roses, a violinist to play Italian love songs, and a candle-lit dinner for two. The light from the candles would flicker in our eyes, reflecting the love that we felt for each other. I would row her across a calm glass-like lake with white swans honking in the distance, under the light of the full moon to the far shore where a blanket had been prepared with a bucket of champaign. We would express our love in words that would make Percy Shelley or Lord Byron envious. She would lay back on the soft blanket, staring up at the stars with me leaning over her, looking deep in her eyes. I would make passionate love to her under the quiet stares of a million stars.

But know I know how foolish and childish this fantasy is.

My writer's imagination has come up with the most romantic, the most perfect fantasy for winning the love of my Sarah Sue. The only fantasy I think could, just possibly, happen:

Johnny Angel would sneak Sarah Sue past his passed out father into the back room of that ramshackle shack he lives in. They would sit on a bed that was more of a cot than a bed with the heat of the furnace scalding the air from the very same room. They would kiss and caress each other. He'd want to get to third base, but Sarah Sue, being a good Catholic girl, would only want to let him hit a double. So he decides, he going for an in-the-park-home-run by raping her.

She breaks from his grasp, kicking him in the crotch, and he collapses into the metal of the furnace burning himself painfully. She runs into the kitchen and gets on the phone, ringing my number, crying for my help before running from the ramshackle shack into the dark of the woods.

I hop on my bicycle and make the several miles to the Clark hovel in a couple of brief moments. Only then do I see Sarah Sue under the bright light of the full moon disappearing into the woods. Johnny runs from his house, his face afire from the scalding pain of the furnace and the pure hatred flushing his face as well. He looks at Sarah Sue vanish into the woods and flicks his switchblade, the steel flashing in the moonlight.

I give chase into the woods and in a small glade I see Johnny standing over Sarah, her dress torn, her breasts exposed to sin. I know that I have to be a man and defend my girl's honor. I call Johnny any number of colorful names to no effect, but when I call him by his Christian name, Eugene, the devil inside his soul shows its awful nature and he turns to stick me.

Sarah screams, begging Johnny not to kill me. I dart and weave, avoiding that painful steel, but

I'm just not fast enough and he slices my hands, my arms, and then sticks me hard. I collapse to the ground, that blade still sticking out of my ribs. My own blood stains the green grass of the once peaceful glade.

My vision blurs, but my hearing is acute. I hear the ripping of her clothes and her muffled cries. She begs for him to stop. Begs him not to do what he is about to do.

But just before he can deflower her virginity with violence, I painfully pull the switchblade from my ribs. With the strength of a risen Lazarus, I rise from my grave and with my bare hands I beat Johnny to death. His cries and screams for mercy echo through the woods, startling sleeping birds enough to take flight. His blood stains my broken hands.

With my newfound strength spent. I collapse to the thankfully soft ground. Sarah Sue looks into my eyes. After she brushes away my tears, I can see "the look" when I look into her eyes. In that moment she actually loves me. Even after tears bead and fall from her eyes, I can still see "the look".

I begin to tell her that I love her, but she puts a finger to my lips and quietly shushes me.

"Good, honest Buddy, be still. Let me say the words. I love you. I have always loved you."

I can now love her, I have her consent to love her back. In that moment we are young lovers with our entire lives ahead of us. Then the Morbid Angel appears and she begs him not to take me. "Now that I know how much I love him, please, don't take him. Not yet. Not until we are both old, having spent out lives together. Please, I need him. Not someone like him. I! Need! Him!"

She loves me in that moment, the moment that I die.

From the Album

Buddy: I pray for death, each and every night.
I can no longer live, I've given up this fight.
I can't take my life, not by my hand,
It's a Mortal Sin, by God's Holy Command.

I pray that a thief with an eye for rape
Will confront us. This is my only escape.

Sarah Sue and I walk alone at night,
I'll defend her honor and die in that fight.

Morbid Angel, Morbid Angel,
Take me away to Heaven Above.
Morbid Angel, Morbid Angel,
Take me away so I'll have her love.

I'll defend her honor to my very death,
With a knife in my ribs, I gasp for breath.
He knocks her down and tears at her clothes,
With evil intent, he tries to deflower her rose.

Like Lazarus, I rise from my grave,
I'll kill this man; Sarah Sue I will save.
With my last breath, I fall into the mud,
Her hands are stained with my blood.

Morbid Angel, Morbid Angel,
Take me away to Heaven Above.
Morbid Angel, Morbid Angel,
Take me away so I'll have her love.

I will love her, with her consent,
She will love me in that moment,
In that moment... with a tear in her eye.
In that moment... she starts to cry.

I will love her, with her consent,

She will love me in that moment,
In that moment... I say goodbye.
In that moment... before I die.

I love you like you're my brother.
As a friend I'd have no other.
You just don't make my heart flutter,
I need someone who is...

Our love is forever, 'till our lives are through
Our love's not the love that you fell into.
That love I won't ever be sharing with you.

I want someone who is...
        Someone like you - but not you - just
        Someone like you - but not you.

Our love wouldn't be real, that I won't pretend.
I'll always   count you a friend.
            always
Until the world comes to a bitter end.
I want someone who is...

I love you in a special way, Buddy Brown.
You're always there when the sun goes down.
You're a great friend who will always be around.
    I want someone who is...
        Someone like you - but not you - just
        Someone like you - but not you.

I need someone to be my best friend.
So our love will never come to an end.
I can't stand the pain of my heart's rend.
I need some one who is...
        Someone like you - but not you - just
        Someone like you - but not you.

I need a lover who is a friend like you.
I need a lover who'll do things a little taboo.
I need a lover who I can have a steamy rendezvous.
I need someone who is...

I want someone who will stay out after curfew.
I want someone who will get a tattoo.
I want someone who's got a little woohoo.
I want someone who is...

Someone like you - but not you - just
Someone like you - BUT NOT YOU.

I need someone who'll always be true.
I need someone who is never really blue.
I need someone who bind my soul with glue.
I need someone who is...

BUDDY BROWN & SARAH SUE
I WAS A TEENAGE ANGEL OF DEATH

SIDE C

1. THE STAIRWAY TO HEAVEN HOP
   i. CLASS OF '57
   ii. ALONE AT THE PUNCHBOWL
   iii. WHEN THE HEART BEGINS TO TALK
   iv. THE NIGHT OF SUPRISES
2. ON THAT FATEFUL NIGHT
3. ON THAT FATEFUL NIGHT - PART 2

Welcome to the Stairway to the Sock Hop
Do-wop- do-do-do-wop, do-wop.
On the dance floor, your feet will drop.
Do-wop, do-do-do-wop, do-wop.
Tonight your teenage hearts will flip-flop.
Do-wop, do-do-do-wop, do-wop.

~~The seniors to the Stairway to Heaven of~~
~~The Stairway~~
The seniors took the Stairway to Heaven
While those of us in the Class of '57.
Stand along the walls and just wait.
Staring across at our lonely dates
We'll never take that step,
It's something we've been to accept.
Never, ever take that chance,
To see if they'd like to dance.
What is it my lonely eyes observe?
One-by-one, we get up the nerve.
Except for me, ol' Buddy Brown.
I look into her eyes and there I'll drown.
My feet are glued to the very spot.
I'm waiting for the music to stop.
I tell myself that, but it's a lie.
I stand there alone and start to cry.

(Chorus)

II

Why am I alone at my own Prom?
Is he sick? Or running late?
I can't stand by the auditorium door,
Is it possible I don't even have a date.

Johnny Angel, seemed to have changed.
But I'm alone, stirring the punch bowl.
He's left me alone at the dance.

It hurts all the way down into my soul.
Why can't I meet a man like Buddy?
Who will be my very, very best friend.
Why can't I meet a man like Buddy?
Why does my love seem like it's at the end?
Johnny Angel, Johnny Angel!
I gave you a second chance.
Johnny Angel, Johnny Angel!
I'm alone at my own dance.

(Chorus)

III

My eyes meet the eyes of Sarah Sue,
My mind and my heart begin to argue
My mind says to haven't a chance.
My heart says ask her to dance.
Do I dare walk over to her?
My courage begins to stir,
Do I offer her my arm? What could be the harm

The Stairway To Heaven Hop

I. CLASS OF '57
From the Journal of Buddy Brown

The Stairway to Heaven is such an arduous ascent that many souls prefer the Coal-Chute to Hell.

I felt like an ocean-liner lost in the North Atlantic and Sarah Sue was the North Star, who would guide me safely through the field of fop-haired icebergs. But she was nowhere to be seen. I knew the fop-haired iceberg would appear without warning and tear a hole in the gymnasium's dance-floor, sending me to the cold, cruel depths of loneliness and despair that would be my life without Sarah Sue Hayes.

The ceiling was lined with clouds of cotton-batting obscuring the star-like balloons and the crowd of fellow students was a low fog rolling in, so I couldn't see the North Star that would light my way out of this ridiculous little story I was telling in my head. Always in my head.

I had hoped my tall stature would allow me to easily spot her standing in the doorway entering the gym, or standing by the punch-bowl getting a glass of that rancid-tasting punch. I didn't know what was wrong with the punch. Had it gone bad sitting out all evening? It was awful, like Baker's chocolate.

I hadn't seen her or Johnny Angel.

I felt a sense of relief that Johnny Angel wasn't here, but my mind began to panic as I realized that if Johnny Angel stood her up, then she wouldn't be in any condition to attend the Prom. And if she wasn't in any condition to attend the Prom, then why in the blue-blazes was I there? Why did I walk that cold, lonely walk to Roncalli if Sarah Sue wasn't going to be here? If she was here, she would have been with Johnny Angel and if she was here with Johnny Angel, then I wouldn't have had a snowball's chance in Hell of wooing her away from him.

I cannot lie to myself and tell myself that I would have tried to take her from him forcefully, with several lightning-fast punches to the face that would leave him lying in a pool of his own blood.

I knew that she would not be here, because Johnny Angel would prove himself to be worthy of his reputation.

Then miraculously Sarah Sue appeared like an angel standing under a light in the gymnasium that shined like the brightest star in the heavens. (I think one of students setting up the gym chose a bulb of several wattage higher than he should have.) I watched from across that remarkably safe gulf that was the hardwood floor of the gymnasium.

But I couldn't shake the feeling that Johnny Angel was parking the car. I couldn't shake the shaking in my knees as I tried to will myself across that dance-floor. My heart pounded so hard in my chest that I thought a voodoo priestess from New Orleans would be drawn to our small steel town to puck it out and save myself from this ridiculous little story I was telling in my head. Always in my head, again.

I would like to think that I would have walked across the dance-floor to stand before Sarah Sue. I would like to think that I took her by the hand and ushered her onto the dance-floor. I would like to think that she rested her head on my once tear-stained shoulder during a wonderfully slow dance-song. I would like to think that I kissed her in that moment. I would like to think that in that moment, she would love me.

I would like to think I hadn't noticed that Jennie Schultz hadn't come up to me and asked me to dance. I would like to think that I hadn't so coldly turned my shoulder to her like she wasn't even there, like she hadn't asked me to dance. I would like to think I wasn't a complete and total schmuck to such a sweet and pretty girl. But I cannot lie. I was such a ▓▓▓▓.

But my life didn't flash before my eyes when Jennie asked me to dance. I didn't see us standing before the Father on our wedding day. I didn't see us having children or growing old together. That is something a chivalrous ▓▓▓▓ imagines. I should have just seen it as a dance. She just wanted to dance. With me. With Mr. Brown. With the booger-eater. All despite me being such a schmuck.

No! I had lost her. I couldn't see my Sarah Sue any more. Where had she gone? I couldn't see Sarah Sue anymore. I had no idea where she could have possibly gone? She was just by the punch-bowl. Where did she go?

Unrequited Lovers:

From the Album
Welcome to the Stairway to Heaven Hop.
Do-wop, do-do-do-wop, do-wop.
On that dance floor, your feet will drop.
Do-wop, do-do-do-wop, do-wop.
Tonight your teenage hearts will flip-flop.
Do-wop, do-do-do-wop, do-wop.

Buddy: *The Seniors took the Stairway to Heaven,*
While those of us in the class of '57,
Stand along the walls and just wait.
Staring across at our lonely dates.

We'll never take that step,
It's something we have to accept.
Never, ever take that chance,
To see if they'd like to dance.

What is it my lonely eyes observe?
One-by-one, we get up the nerve.
Except for me, ol' Buddy Brown,
I look into her eyes and there I drown.

My feet are glued to the very spot,
I'm waiting for the music to stop.
I tell myself that, but it's just a lie.
I stand there alone and start to cry.

Unrequited Lovers: *Welcome to the Stairway to Heaven Hop.*
Do-wop, do-do-do-wop, do-wop.
Our music won't come to a complete stop.
Do-wop, do-do-do-wop, do-wop.
So dance and dance until you all drop.
Do-wop, do-do-do-wop, do-wop.

II. ALONE AT THE PUNCHBOWL

From Sarah Sue's Diary

Dear Diary,

I can't believe writing in you can be so blessedly cathartic.

I can't believe that Johnny, no Eugene, stood me up for the Prom. As I sat on the edge of my bed, waiting for my date, my boyfriend, my everything as he would walk up the walk and ring the door bell, I pined for the evening we were going to have together. Johnny Angel would never be caught dead at a school dance. But it was Eugene Clark who asked his girlfriend, Sarah Sue Hayes to the Prom. When I would have heard the door-bell chime, I would stand and straighten my dress, slowly open my bedroom door, and with much pomp-and-circumstance walk to the top of the stairs. I would look down as my date, my boyfriend, my everything as he looked up at me with love in those big, blue, Frankie Sinatra eyes of his. With each tread I would take, my heart would quicken its beat, until I reached the landing. Eugene would reach his hand out and take mine in his. Like a knight in his newly pressed tuxedo, he would kiss my hand, before pinning the flowered corsage to my wrist. Eugene would ask my father's permission to take his youngest daughter to the dance. My father would smile his appreciation that Eugene was being a true gentleman. Eugene would open the passenger-side door of his father's impossible corvette, as we set out on the greatest, grandest adventure of all, the Prom.

I can't believe that Mrs. Brown had to drive me to my Prom. I sat on the bottom-step weeping like a child who just discovered that Santa Claus wasn't real; that I had placed all my hopes and dreams on a phantasm. My mother was so concerned for my well-being, my sanity, that she went over to the Brown's house to ask if Buddy would be willing to drive the two us to the Prom. Mrs. Brown apologized to my mother. Buddy had already left for the school; he had walked to the Prom. He needed the air to build up his courage to ask some girl, any girl, to dance. But Mrs. Brown offered to drive me to the school, to which my mother politely declined. My father threatened to kill Eugene, no Johnny Angel, if he ever showed his blankedly-blank behind at our door again. But I allowed Mrs. Brown to drive to me to the Prom.

I can't believe I'm at my Prom alone. When I walked into the gymnasium, decorated so beautifully with its paper-ribbon streamers, helium-filled balloons lining the ceiling like starlight, cotton batting pinned to the rafters like white fluffy clouds, a shakingly constructed "Stairway to Heaven", and a band of misfit college-students playing in their "rock'n' roll" band. I couldn't happen but smile at the sight of the boys standing along the north wall like Pall-bearers at a funeral, strangely, their own funeral. And along the south wall, the girls gossiped quietly about the couples who had had the courage to actually step onto the dance floor to dance. Our adult chaperones tried to convince us to dance, but we were as unwilling as we were unable.

I slipped over to the refreshment table and sipped on a glass of punch. I instantly realized that someone, some senior, had spiked the punch-bowl with rum.

I can't believe I drank four glasses of punch.

I can't believe I slipped out of the Prom, unable as I was unwilling to dance with anyone other than my Eugene. I imagined, as I walked down the lowly halls of Roncalli High, that Eugene had had issues borrowing his father's car, that Eugene had had been caught on the other side of the tracks by an unusually long train, that Eugene had had pulled up at my house just as Mrs. Brown and I drove off, that Eugene had had to survive my father's wrath to drive to the Prom to catch up with me. But none of this had happened. I was alone at my Prom.

I can't believe that I went to my locker to retrieve a note-book so I can write these words down. I don't understand how an English class assignment is lifting my spirits from the depths of hell for being stupid enough to be at the Stairway to Heaven Hop alone. Buddy had sang the praises of this stupid assignment, but I saw it as nothing but a painful reminder of the misery I have suffered at the hands of my father, and at the hands of Eugene, no Johnny Angel.

Can this stupid diary be my stairway to Heaven?

I can't believe I am sitting in the girl's bathroom, hidden in the last stall, writing these words down. I can hear the girls gossiping like nagging old hens about why this girl wore that dress to Prom, about doesn't this girl know dancing with that boy with knock her a few rungs down the popularity ladder, about that nose-picker Mr. Brown had the nerve to show up to the senior Prom, alone.

Buddy...

"How dare he", they cackled just on the other side of the door to the bathroom stall.

"Where was that poor girl he was always so thick-as-thieves with?"

"Oh," one of the lesser hens said as the brood leaned in closer to hear, "She finally, months back, got a few cents of good sense to - thank God - drop him!"

The brood continued to cackle.

I have a few good cents to beat some sense into those gossiping old hens, but my feet are glued to the linoleum. I am either unable or unwilling to move.

I can't believe my thoughts are turning to poor, lonely Buddy standing by his lonesome all alone along the wall of the gymnasium. I haven't thought about him since that night when he confessed his love for me. This is a lie. Mrs. Story, you would be so ashamed of me. The Father would be so ashamed of me. That wee-little devil that sits on my shoulder would be so ashamed me that he would refuse to tempt me any longer; he would tell the Devil that I was the evilest thing in all creation. I think about Buddy the moment I wake up in the morning, the moment I cry myself to sleep, the moment I bolt upright in bed after surviving a nightmare. I've tried to convince myself that Eugene is the only thing I think about. That is what love is, isn't it? Being unable to get someone out of their mind; being unwilling to live another day without that person in your life; being unable to imagine your life without that person being in there somewhere; being unwilling to allow the past...

I can't believe that I am going to live my life without Buddy in it. I always imagined Buddy standing in the front pew during my Wedding Mass. I always imagined Buddy sitting in the waiting room at the hospital, comforting my husband as I gave birth for my first child. I always imagined Buddy being Godfather to my child, my children. I had always imagined Buddy comforting me at my husband's funeral. I always imagined Buddy and I sitting on the porch of his house, reminiscing on the quality lives we lived. I always imagined my life with Buddy Brown in it somewhere.

And then I go and ruin it like I always do.

How many times in the months since that fate-filled night when all went hay-wire have I wondered about all the times that Buddy wanted to tell me he was in love with me but wouldn't, no couldn't tell me. What must it be like to have those kinds of feelings, but never have the courage to say them? Why would Buddy prefer to live his life as my brother instead of my lover? I now know why. I was unable, no unwilling to accept that kind of love. It would be too overwhelming, that kind of love. I'd rather be treated like a piece of dog ████, than be treated like a lady should be. Where is the danger in that life? There would be none. There could be none. There should be none.

I can't believe I am feeling the feelings I am feeling.

I can't believe I am about to go looking for my best friend. I can't believe...

From the Album

Sarah Sue: *Why am I alone at my own Prom?*
Is he sick? Or running a little late?
I can't stand by the auditorium doors,
Is it possible I don't even have a date?

Johnny Angel seemed to have changed,
But I'm alone, stirring the punch bowl.
He's left me all alone at the dance.
It hurts all the way down into my soul.

Why can't I meet a man like Buddy,
Who will be my very, very best friend.
Why can't I meet a man like Buddy,
Why does my life seem like it's at the end?

Johnny Angel, Johnny Angel,
I gave you a second chance.
Johnny Angel, Johnny Angel.
I'm alone at my own dance.

Unrequited Lovers: *Welcome to the Stairway to Heaven Hop.*
                 Do-wop, do-do-do-wop, do-wop.
       That little girl's date didn't bother to show up.
                 Do-wop, do-do-do-wop, do-wop.
       She cries and cries, her tears won't seem to stop.
                 Do-wop, do-do-do-wop, do-wop.

III. WHEN THE HEART BEGINS TO TALK

From the Journal of Buddy Brown

When I couldn't find my Sarah Sue in the endless sea of students, I would have thought that a panic would overtake my heart. Why wasn't I panicking? I wanted my heart to beat itself to death, so that I could die.

Strangely, I felt at peace. It was not a heavenly kind of peace that my soul no longer felt any pangs of love towards my best friend. I felt the reservation that a convict feels as he walks towards the electric-chair, the kind of peace knowing that the endless pain will soon be over.

I needed to let her go. I needed to accept the fact that Sarah Sue would never love me in the way that I deserved to be loved. I needed to resign myself to a life without Sarah Sue in it.

I needed that long walk home in the cold, spring evening to keep myself from jumping to my death into the cold river's depths, when I got to the bridge.

I walked towards the gymnasium doors to, as quietly as I could, exit the Prom without anyone noticing me. But I wasn't that lucky. As I looked down at my spit-shined shoes, I felt the cold, icy stares of my classmates. My Dumbo-sized ears caught the chatter of their gossip that I couldn't find any girl willing to dance with Mr. Brown, that booger-eater.

I needed to escape that throng of students, who had tormented me throughout my academic-career. I hated them as much as they hated me, although my hatred was entirely justified. I had done nothing to them, but they had done everything to me: swirlies, purple-nurples, Indian-rug-burns. I suffered through their incessant gossip, their undeserved taunts, their relentless beatings. I stood there and, for the first time in my life, gave them permission to hate me. I wanted them, no needed them to think I was a complete and total loser. I needed them to hate me more than I hated myself. If I could just project my self-loathing into unrivaled anger towards my classmates, then I might survive this night. I was about to lift a middle-finger to the entire lot of them (let them gossip about that while I was suspended for the next several days), but I kept my composure.

As I exited through the doors into the cold, windy night, I turned towards their glares, to soak in the heat of their loathing towards me. I would need that heat if I was to survive my long walk home. I stood there just long enough to see Sarah Sue walk into the gymnasium from the inner bowels of the school.

Normally, I would have turned tail and ran as far away as I could, but I had gotten my Irish up. The heat of those cold, icy stares ignited a fire in my heart. I was not going to let them stop me. I was not going to let me stop me.

The cold, glassy North sea of students parted as I walked forward with such determination they were left stunned in my wake. Sarah Sue seemed oblivious to the murmurs of the crowd, as she again stood under that over-wattaged light. It must have seemed like I appeared out of the fog of students, because she was slightly startled when her eyes caught mine. I still couldn't see that spark in her eyes when she looked at me, but she smiled and that was enough.

The shear brashness of my actions scared me. The fire that raged in my chest overwhelmed any argument that my mind wanted to quarrel with. I took Sarah Sue's hand into mine and I led her onto the dance-floor. A shyness crept over her face as her eyes dropped to the floor and then sheepishly raised her eyes to look into mine. But she followed me into the middle of the floor. The walk was the walk of eternity. The walk towards the future I had always imagined my life living.

From the Album

Buddy:
My eyes meet the eyes of Sarah Sue,
My mind and my heart begin to argue.
My mind says I haven't a chance.
My heart says ask her to dance.

Do I dare walk over to her?
My courage begins to stir.
Do I offer her my arm?
What could be the harm?

The walk is a long walk,
My mind begins to balk.
The walk is such a long walk,
When my heart begins to talk.

This is my very last chance,
"Sarah Sue, would you like to dance?"
Maybe she sees I'm more than a friend,
I hope, I hope, this song ever ends.

Unrequited Lovers: *Welcome to the Stairway to Heaven Hop.*
Do-wop, do-do-do-wop, do-wop.
Buddy Brown, don't you dare stop.
Do-wop, do-do-do-wop, do-wop.
Buddy Brown, don't you dare stop.
Do-wop, do-do-do-wop, do-wop.

IV. A NIGHT OF SURPRISES

From the Journal of Buddy Brown

When the song, that song I never imagined would be played, began to play, there were tears in her eyes. I wasn't entirely sure if they were tears she had previously cried over Johnny Angel having stood her up at her prom. Her cheeks had been streaked red with those tears of sorrow, but these seemed to be tears of joy. Were these tears actually tears of love? The lights hanging from the rafters of the gymnasium danced in her tears and for a moment, I believed them to be that spark that I had longed to see from a girl.

When she wiped the tears from her eyes, she silently whispered, "I'm sorry" as she rested her head on my shoulder, her tears staining my shoulder again. I heard Sarah Sue sniffle. I heard Sarah Sue sob. But I couldn't believe that they were tears of sorrow, but tears of joy. She nuzzled her head more snug into my shoulder and her arms squeezed me tightly.

I thanked God for this moment, even if it would be a fleeting one.

But it didn't seem to be so fleeting. When the song ended, I thought we would part, perhaps for eternity, but she didn't let me go, wouldn't let me go. She still clung to me as if our parting would mean our deaths. Our hearts were beating as one. We took our breaths in unison. We were becoming...

I don't know.

She lifted her head from my shoulder. She apologized for being a mess. She reached into her clutch-purse to retrieve her handkerchief to wipe her face. After that eternity of a moment, she looked up at me with that "look". There was definitely a spark in her eyes. I stepped in towards her and she welcomed my presence, our eyes never parting our loving stare. Sarah leaned into towards me to kiss me on the lips. I bent downwards to meet her lips with mine...

We kissed.

In that moment, I understood the mysteries of Creation. I knew why God had created Man and Woman. I understood the Sacrament of Marriage for the first time. Truly understood. As a young Altar Boy, I had witnessed the Marriage Mass on numerous occasions, but I never understood it. I never truly understood it. When the priest would join the couple together in the bounds of Holy Matrimony, he would end the vows with, "You may now kiss the bride." My reaction to the beautiful moment that drove grown adults to tears was innocent child-like revulsion. Ewww. I couldn't understand why they would kiss. I knew that when I got married, I would kiss my wife for the first and only time. As a child, one is stuck in the eternal school-yard quandary, girls are gross, yet at the same time strangely alluring. A boy knew that one day he would grow up, get married, and have children. How exactly this happened and why, well that was something to worry about another day. Today was for digging up worms.

When Sarah Sue and I kissed, I truly understood another mystery of matrimony: the two bodies becoming one. My naïveté, even as a teenager, could not comprehend how two bodies could become one body; how two souls could become one soul. I may have wanted to become one with Sarah Sue in marriage and in life, but nothing in my lonely existence had prepared me to completely comprehend this. But when our lips met, I truly understood the union of a man and his wife. God had answered my question of why He gave us the gift of this sacrament. I could feel my soul merging with her's. We breathed as one. Our hearts beat as one. We were one.

But in that moment, in that ever so brief and fleeting moment, Buddy and Sarah Sue were the perfect pair. Sarah Sue was as much mine as I was hers.

As we kissed, our life together flashed before my eyes, in the most wonderful of ways.

I saw...

The harsh squealing of feedback from the microphone, pulled Sarah and I out of our moment. A moment that had been ours and ours alone. A moment that should have lasted until eternity. But the principal of the school, Mr. Schultz, took to the microphone to announce that Johnny Angel had been shot.

From the Album

Buddy:
Her eyes are filled with tears,
It's something I haven't seen in years.
Is this my one and only chance?
And we begin our first dance.

She wipes the tears from her eyes,
Her heart seems to apologize.
She rests her head on my shoulder.
All I have to do is… hold her.

There are tear stains on my shoulder
Buddy Brown, you just have to hold her.
The love's seed is growing into a tree.
Her love is blossoming, just wait and see.

I hold her gently on the hips,
She leans in to kiss me on the lips,
There is definitely a spark in her eyes.
… … … … … … …
Then we are both given a unwelcome surprise!

Unrequited Lovers:
The Stairway to Heaven Hop,

Do-wop, do-do-do-wop, do-wop.
Came to a sudden and abrupt stop.
Do-wop, do-do-do-wop, do-wop.
Johnny Angel, he has been shot.
Do-wop, do-do-do-what?

From the Journal of Buddy Brown

Sarah Sue clunged to me, not out of the love and sincerity that was just so fleetingly there for a moment, but in the fear and horror of the reality that her Johnny Angel has been shot. Her fingers dug into my back as her legs weakened. I held her up with my body and my words. I told her it would be okay. I told her that everything would be okay.

I lied to her.

I knew that everything wasn't going to okay, but I said those words to comfort her. I knew that this was going to be the most difficult thing Sarah Sue had ever experienced. She had survived the beatings of her father a stronger woman. She had survived the two-timing of Johnny Angel with another woman. But this... The woman she was just a few moments ago had died with the realization that her Johnny Angel was dead. The woman who had just loved me in the precious few moments moments earlier was already a drastically different creature. The woman who would continue to live would be nothing but a shell of her former self.

As much as I hated Johnny Angel for everything he did to Sarah Sue and, to a lesser extent, to me, I don't believe I ever wished him death. Mrs. Story, I may be wrong (this journal being proof), but I don't want to believe I wished him death. I would have given up my life for Sarah Sue, but I never would have wished death on anyone else.

Sarah Sue's quiet, loving tears had metamorphosed into a torrent of weeping and wailing. I combed my fingers through her hair. My words tried to sooth her unbearable grief, but I would not be able quiet her suffering. It was her's and nobody, myself included, could suffer it for her.

I just needed to be there for her. As I always had been and always would be.

As her knees buckled under the weight of her grief, my knees bent as well. I held her in my arms. I felt through her weeps and sobs that our hearts were beating differently, at a different pace. Her's was rapid and shuttering, while mine was painfully slow and at peace. I knew in that moment our hearts would never again beat as one. Her heart was breaking and like a broken clock it would never again tick like all other clocks. A broken clock doesn't keep time anymore. Her heart would never again be in sync with mine.

As our classmates stared at us, their eyes and mouths agape, the ring of students around us widened as the realization that Johnny Angel was dead. The gossiping and the rumor-mongering became deathly quiet. Disturbingly so.

Mr. Schultz fumbled with his keys as he opened the door to the front office, so that I could call my mother to come get Sarah Sue and me. The ride home seemed to take years. While Sarah Sue held onto me, she did not allow her grip to lessen on my hopefully comforting body. As her bottomless well of tears stained my shoulder, I knew the gulf between us remained infinite. I feared that by morning, she would not remember our kiss we shared, our moment together, when our undying love died.

On That Fateful Night

From the Journal of Buddy Brown

Why?

Why did the love that Sarah Sue and I shared so beautifully on the dance-floor of the "Stairway to Heaven Hop" die in same moment that Johnny Angel was lying dying in the hospital of the nearby city? As he gasped for his final breaths, Sarah Sue was gasping through her sobs and her wails.

What were the events that led to his death and the ruin of so many lives?

The county sheriff had found a "diary" (how, Johnny Angel would have loathed him using that word) that had outlined the events of that evening, as Johnny Angel had orchestrated it. Unfortunately for Johnny and for Sarah Sue, his plans didn't go as, well, planned.

The Sheriff was so uncouth that he showed Johnny Angel's diary to Sarah Sue. He made her read the words that Johnny had written to see if she had any foreknowledge of the events of that evening. As if she was an accomplice? Sarah Sue had to find out that Johnny was going to propose marriage to her at her Prom in his "confession" to armed robbery.

This is how she found out!

From the "Secret" Journal of Johnny Angel

Misses Story will hate that I am using this stupid diary of her's to plan out this evening of mine. First and foremost, I want the police to know, if this all goes bad, that I don't want anybody to get hurt. I'm just going to walk into the liquor store and take seventy-five dollars, the exact amount of money that I need to buy back my mother's wedding ring that has been sitting in the pawn shop for the last several years. I hate my old man for hocking her ring, having stolen it off her lifeless hand. She should have been buried with that ring on her finger, instead of sitting unsold, unwanted, in the display-case of a filthy pawn shop. My old man said they had vowed "until death do us part" so in death she should be parted with that so-called bobble.

How that hate my old man.

I am going to ride my bike out into the county where there is a liquor store out in the boonies that nobody I know goes in. It closes at five in the evening for heaven's sake. What kind of town closes down at five in the evening? And what kind of town that closes down at five in the evening has a liquor store? You're think it would be all Christianed up. Even our little podunk town stays open until at least nine. There shouldn't be anybody in there at closing time. There shouldn't be any hassle with the old lady that runs the place, 'cause her husband runs the general store down the road a bit. One of my Rebel Angels had already sticked them up in the past (and to the Sheriff, no I ain't going to name names, not here at least). So I know I'm in the clear.

Once I have the money, I'm going to head over to that piece of ▄▄▄ pawn shop and buy back my dear sweet momma's wedding ring. You may be asking yourself, Sheriff, why don't I just rob the pawn shop. First, it's just down the rode from my old man's house. Second, that old codger who runs the place knows I want my momma's ring. I've tried to haggle down the price so I could buy it legit so many times that that ██████ing ██████ won't work with me anymore. He knows I want it, so he wants to put me through the wringer to get my momma's ring back. Seventy-five dollars cold hard cash or no deal. If I rob him, he will know it is me that steals that ring and I'll end up standing before a judge, instead of before the altar with my sweet Sarah Sue marrying me. So I'm going to buy it as legit as I can, even if that means robbing a liquor store.

Is that what you would call irony, Misses Story?

Then I am going to drive to the Hayes' house to escort my future fianceé (Misses Story would be proud I got that right) to her Prom. I know that a true gentleman asks her father for his permission for her hand in marriage, but I seriously don't think even if I ask him in the privacy of his study that he would, never in a million years, agree. I also don't think Sarah Sue would hold it against me for not asking an abusive ██████ing ██████, so I'm going to be a cad by not asking his permission.

In my imagination, I can see Sarah Sue walk down the staircase, staring down at me in the ridiculous powder-blue tux with that radiant smile of her's melting my greasy heart. I'll pin that flower-thing to her wrist like I'm supposed to and I'll walk her to my father's car and we'll head off for the Prom.

Once there, I'm going to slip a fiver to the band to play our song. I'm going to lead her to the middle of the dance-floor, with all of the students staring at us, all those people who I couldn't care less about were going to witness something they would never forget. For the rest of their traditional nine-to-five lives, they are going to puzzle over my actions. What did Johnny Angel do that night?

After slow-dancing with my girl resting her head on my shoulder, as the song winds down, I'm going to bend down onto one knee. I hope she has tears of joy in her eyes as the realization of what I'm about to do washes over her like a warm spring rain. Then, I'm going to reach into my pocket and retrieve my momma's wedding ring (the one thing in my old man's life that he actually got right). After opening that box with a loud crack, with the light of that diamond dancing in her eyes, I'm going to pop the question. I'm going to ask Sarah Sue Hayes to become Mrs. Eugene Clark.

By the end of the night Johnny Angel will be dead. Dead and buried in the cemetary of teenage rebelliousness. This is going to be a rebirth for me. Eugene Francis Clark.

From the Journal of Buddy Brown

What happened that fateful night, however, was much, much different. I'm sure it never occurred to Johnny that the evening was not going to go as he planned. I've always puzzled over how people think they are going to get away with "it". He had to have known that something could have, and probably would go wrong. He was going to commit a criminal act (not the first in his sorry life, but hopefully it would have been the last).

When Johnny Angel set out for that hamlet, how would he know that the priest of the county parish buys his Communion wine for Sunday Mass at closing time Saturday evening? He had survived D-Day's relentless horror, after which he became an conscientious objector and a Catholic priest. He faithfully served his country on the European front until the end of the war. This was one priest who would not have been fazed by the sight of a gun being pointed at him; not only did he survive a war, his soul was already bought and paid for by Christ upon the cross.

(I never learnt the priest's name, but I'll call him Monseigneur Bienvenu for lack of a better name. Mrs. Story, are you proud I remember my *Les Misérables?*)

How was Johnny Angel supposed to know that when one of his Rebel Angels had stolen a bottle of whiskey, a couple of packs of smokes, and rifled through the cash-register, that that was the impetus for the husband, who ran the general store, to buy his wife a shotgun out of fear of "some greasy-haired punk with a lady's gun"?

How was Johnny Angel supposed to know that St. Michael, the patron saint of police officers, had sent a young sheriff's deputy to the liquor store to buy a small bottle of whiskey to sooth his infant son's teething pains and the young mother's nerves?

How was Johnny Angel supposed to know that he would get nowhere near Roncalli High that evening? How was Johnny Angel supposed to know that my mother had driven Sarah Sue to the Prom. How was Johnny Angel supposed to know that his little adventure would destroy not only his life, but the lives of everyone in it? How was Johnny Angel supposed to know that while he lay dying, Sarah Sue's lips were locked onto mine?

The sight of a young man, with newly cut hair and wearing a rented powder-blue tuxedo and two-toned shoes, must have been seen as the strangest of sights during an armed robbery. It must have given the old lady behind the counter pause, thinking this was a prank of some kind. But it was real. All too real. An actual armed robbery.

I'm sure that Monseigneur Bienvenu tried talk Johnny out of the committing this crime. The priest would have given him some Catholic mumbo-jumbo (at least in Johnny's mind it would be) about breaking a mortal sin and the threats of eternal damnation; that if he changed his mind and walked back out of the door, there wouldn't have been a crime committed. Johnny would only be guilty of the sin of intention. He would be forgiven for his intentions to rob the liquor story, if only he would confess before the priest as a man of God and ask for the Lord's forgiveness. And it would be not only offered, but given. What would drive a young man in the prime of his life, wearing a nice tuxedo to rob a liquor store?

Johnny, apparently, confessed to the priest he needed to buy his momma's wedding ring so he would propose to his sweetheart at the Prom. The Monseigneur asked the old lady behind the counter to put his wine for Sunday mass on credit, so he could give this young man all of the money he had, which he hoped would be enough to help this young man out. The owner protested, but Bienvenu insisted. He had just handed Johnny Angel four twenty-dollar bills, when the sheriff's deputy, fatefully walked into the liquor store.

The deputy must have seen a young man being handed a wad of bills by the county priest, all while holding a gun in his right hand.

I can only imagine next few moments played out like the shoot-out at the OK corral as filmed by the Three Stooges: the deputy went for his weapon, Johnny's gun went off in his hand, the old lady grabbed her shot-gun, pointed in the general direction of Johnny Angel and fired. Gunfire thundered and glass and liquor rained down and in the end, the priest lay bleeding on the floor. And Johnny had disappeared like a fart in a whirlwind.

The deputy heard the signature growl of the Harley's V-Twin and ran out into a sudden rain and down half-a-block to the police box on a pole by the gas-pumps to call for back up. Soon, flashing lights and sirens would echo like lightning and thunder through that fateful night.

From the Album

Buddy:
On that fateful night,
Johnny did what he thought right,
To win the heart of his girl,
He'd take on the entire world.
He'd do just about anything,
To give his girl her a wedding ring.

Johnny walked into a liquor store,
And ordered everyone on the floor.
He pulled a ski-mask over his head,
And told everyone that they'd be dead.

If they tried to lift nary a finger,
He'd put them through the wringer.
But a passing patrol man saw Johnny.
Breakin' that 5th Commandment-sin.

He ran down to the police-box,
Johnny's life just hit the hard knocks.
Soon the sirens would begin to wail,
And poor old Johnny would go to jail.

On that fateful night,
Johnny did what he thought right,
To win the heart of his girl,
He'd take on the entire world.
He'd do just about anything,
To give his girl her a wedding ring.

Johnny stole the money out of the drawer,
And was chased out of the back door.
Johnny jumped on his motorcycle,
The officer said a quick prayer to St. Michael.

Then hopped in his car to give chase.
And down Main Street there's quite a race.
Johnny raced towards his side of the tracks,
He knew he had to win his girl back.

He had to get to the pawn shop,
There's nothing could make him stop.
He needed to buy his mother's ring,
The flashing lights lit up the evening.

On that fateful night,
Johnny did what he thought right,

To win the heart of his girl,
He'd take on the entire world.
He'd do just about anything,
To give his girl her a wedding ring.

On That Fateful Night

From Sarah Sue's Diary

Dear Diary,

Why?

Why did Eugene walk into that liquor store? What was he thinking? The words he wrote in his journal, now stained with my tears, offer little understanding, but a world of explanation. I read not only what he wrote of his intentions, but the entire journal, from the beginning of the year until this fateful night. He had gone to his grave having not answered a single question I had had. It only posed more unanswerable questions.

Why didn't Eugene just buy me any old ring? Why did he get it in his thick skull that only his momma's ring would do? Why didn't he just send in some cereal box tops and put Little Orphan Anne's decoder ring on my finger? I would have said "Yes" to an empty jewelry box.

I didn't need any old bobble (how Johnny is cursing me from Heaven to use that word to describe his momma's wedding ring), but I don't want any old ring to be Mrs. Eugene Clark. I just need Eugene Clark.

Eugene Clark died the moment he walked into the liquor store, it would take a several more horrifying minutes for Johnny Angel to die. Even if he had been successful in robbing that liquor store, even if he had been successful in reaching that pawn shop to buy back his momma's wedding ring, even if he had showed up at the prom and gotten down on bended me to propose to me, I wouldn't have married him once I discovered the most precious ring in the world, my engagement ring from Eugene Clark was the project of ill-gotten gains. How could any woman wear such a symbol on her hand?

I hate Eugene or Johnny or whoever the Hell just died tonight. I hate him for loving me so much that his only choice was committing that awful sin. I hate him so much for shooting a priest, who still clings to life in the room next to where Johnny died. I hate him so much because that kind priest, through his own gasps for breath, gave Johnny his Last Rites through the plaster wall separating them.

I hate him. I hate him. I hate him.

I know what happened that night. The police have explained it to me in such gruesome detail. I know they think I was an accomplice to my own marriage proposal, which is now a criminal investigation. How in the name of Judas Priest is that even a justification to turn my entire world upside down? How dare they think that I would have been part of my Johnny committing a robbery.

I know the life I am now forced to live all because Johnny walked into that liquor store. I know what could have happened that night if Johnny had been successful. I know that I would have said yes. I know that I would have let him put that ring on my finger. I know what I would want to live the rest of my life without ever knowing the awful truth about this fateful night. I know that would want to go to my grave in complete and blessed ignorance. Only to know the truth when I stood before the Lord as He read from the book of life.

Which life would I have wanted to live? The life where I married a criminal? Or the life where I buried a criminal? Strange where poetry and rhyme seem to appear magically out of the ether, huh, Mrs. Story?

The words written in that awful police report were so cold and mechanical that I dare not remember those words when I reminisce on the final moments of my Johnny's life.

This is not how I will remember how my Johnny died.

From the Album

Sarah Sue:
> *On that fateful night,*
> *My Johnny did what he thought right,*
> *To win the heart of his girl,*
> *He'd take on the entire world.*
> *He'd do just about anything,*
> *To give me a wedding ring.*
>
> *But on the tracks was a passing train,*
> *That he would try to beat it was insane,*
> *The end of this story there is no like,*
> *My Johnny crashed his motorbike.*
>
> *Which burst into an inferno of flame.*
> *The Angel of Death took down his name.*
> *The Fates don't often play very nice,*
> *My Johnny's blood run as cold as ice.*
>
> *Cause he survived that fiery crash.*
> *But the law was still on his ass.*
> *That police officer pulled his gun,*

And my Johnny, he tried… to run.

No, Johnny, no!

> On that fateful night,
> Johnny did what he thought right,
> To win the heart of his girl,
> He'd take on the entire world.
> He'd do just about anything,
> To give me a wedding ring.

That police called for Johnny to stop,
Then he fired at my Johnny a single shot,
The bullet pierced the flesh of his back,
And he fell down on now empty set of tracks.

Other police officers soon came around,
My Johnny's blood soaked into the cold hard ground.
"I know that tonight, I acted the fool,
But I've got to get to my High School.

I've got to propose to my Sarah Sue,
Please, let me go, I'm begging you."
This was all my Johnny ever said,
Because, after that moment…

My Johnny was dead…

BUDDY BROWN & SARAH SUE
I WAS A TEENAGE ANGEL OF DEATH

SIDE D

1. THE NOTE
2. DEATH ANGEL
3. HEALING DOES COME
4. LIKE IT WAS YESTERDAY (Reprise)

Death Angel, Death Angel,
Why did you answer her call?

Death Angel, Death Angel,
I'd have been there, if she should fall.
I'd have washed her scraped knee,
I'd have done anything she needed of me.

Death Angel, Death Angel,
Why did you walk into her home
Death Angel, Death Angel,
Couldn't you have left her alone?
I'd have nursed her through her pain.
The sun wouldn't shine through the rain

Death Angel, Death Angel,
Did you stand there when she slit her wrists?

Death Angel, Death Angel,
Couldn't you have crossed her name off your list.
Couldn't you leave her alone with me?
Couldn't you leave her be?

Death Angel, Death Angel!
You took the only girl I'll ever love.
Death Angel, Death Angel,
I know you saw the one above.
But let them know starting tonight
I'll never ever again be all right.

Death Angel, Death Angel.
You won't see me for a long time
Death Angel, Death Angel.
You see I haven't committed a crime.
Except the crime of loving someone.
My life isn't over, in fact...
            it's just begun.

SIDE D - SONG 1

The Note

From Sarah Sue's Diary

I know that Buddy Brown has been secretly writing songs on a guitar which he claims he doesn't know a lick about. I know that Buddy is a far more accomplished guitarist than he lets on or would even admit to himself. I've sat under my windowsill with the window open listening to him play his songs through his ever-open window. His songs are beautiful. They are so magical and pure. Even before that night he professed his undying love for me, I have sat quietly across the gulf between our two windows, listening to him pick the words out of the ether and pick the notes one after another until they finally sang. I have shed many a tear listening to how he has captured our lives so poetically and truthfully. How he is able to distill an entire life into only a few words is miraculous. How he captured his undying love for me is hearth-wrenching.

I know that I will be immortalized in the songs that Buddy Brown will write. Thousands of young girls will listen to his album and imagine that they are the object of Buddy Brown's affections. They will wish that they could be the woman Sarah Sue never was. These poor girls will promise that if Buddy Brown were only to love them and only them, Buddy Brown's love for them would not be unrequited. Their fantasies will be filled with such foolish fancies. They will swoon at his concerts, scream like banshees when he sings, and clutch and claw at him like Harpies as he rushes to his touring bus after the concert. They will stalk him at his hotels and along the highways. They want to be the one to heal Buddy's heart of his "Heartache Hangover". But I go to my grave knowing that I am Sarah Sue, the girl who broke Buddy Brown's heart. I go into the loving caress of death knowing that I will be immortalized in the songs that will make Buddy Brown a Rock 'n' Roll star. I will continue to live in his words and in his music long after I have "shuffled off this mortal coil". (Yes, Mrs. Story, I remember my Shakespeare.)

I must admit, Diary, that when I heard the words to his song, "Someone Like You (But Not You)" that I died a little bit inside, because I never fully realized how much words can hurt. Yes, my father's words have stung me so many times, that I shudder to remember them at all. But my father was vicious with his words. He had intended his words to hurt. I never imagined that words spoken with ignorant innocence could be barbed. That my barbed words would wrap themselves around his heart and with each and every beat, would inflict the most pain imaginable on him.

There is a little bottle of pills in the medicine cabinet in the bathroom off of the master bedroom that has been sitting quietly and patiently since my Johnny beat the loving tar out of my father. My father is old-fashioned and doesn't believe in popping pills to ease his pain. Only women "pop pills". He would take his beating like a man. He would drink his way through the pain. It would be a sign of weakness to take any those blasted pills that the doctor insisted in writing a prescription for and my mother insisted the pharmacist fill. Now, those pills whose sole purpose in this life is to alleviate unimaginable suffering and they will accomplish their life's work when they put me out of my unimaginable suffering.

I'm going to lay this diary down in a few moments. I've already clutched that bottle of pills to my chest as I write my final thoughts. I'm not going to hide these words anymore. I'm no longer going to ask Buddy Brown to secret them away in the safety of his room. I'm going to leave them for the world to see. When my mother finds my body in the morning, she will have all of the answers to her questions. I'm not going to leave questioned unanswered like my Johnny did.

Mom, I'm sorry that you are the one who is going to find me.

Dad... I've got nothing I want to say to you.

Johnny, I'll see you in a few moments.

Buddy, I hope when you have graduated and moved away to attend college that you forget about me and only remember me when you perform those songs I've so enjoyed listening to. Go to those hip and trendy coffee bars and shed this post-war generation that has grown so fearful and tepid for a more lively and upBeat generation. I hope you meet a producer to record your songs and a label to immortalize them in wax.

I have written a song that I hope you, my dearest Buddy Brown, will include on the album you are writing. I hope that you will be able to pull the music out of the mysterious ether you so beautifully commune with. I hope that you, my dearest Buddy Brown, will sing this song one day in remembrance of me. I hope that you will be able to marry your music to my words. I'm sorry this is the only marriage I am capable of giving you.

I love you.

Now, Buddy this is the time to turn the page and let go... of... me...

THE NOTE
by Sarah Sue Hayes

Dearest Angel of Death,
Please come and take my last breath.
I loved my Johnny like I loved no other,
With all my sobs, I feel that I'll smother.
I can no longer stand this mortal pain.
Hell's fire will sooth like spring's rain.
The torment from the devils of the pit,
Is easier to bear than school-mate gossip.
I'll never love another like my Johnny Angel,
I'll toll the bell that sounds my death knell.
The tears don't seem like they'll ever end.
Should I… should I turn to my best friend?

My Dearest Buddy Brown,
Why do I feel like I'm going to drown?
I know that you would save my life,
But I'd cause you nothing but strife.
I know you love me with your whole heart,
If I tried to love you, I'd tear your soul apart.
You need to find another one to love,
Find someone who fits you like a glove.
Find someone who will always be true.
You will find your true love… out of the blue.
I'm nearing the final bars of my life's song.
Please, don't shed a tear for me… when I'm gone.

SIDE D - SONG 2

Death Angel

From the Journal of Buddy Brown

The Angel of Death waltzed his way into my life and I didn't even know it. As I sat under the sill of my window picking away at my guitar, just a few feet away and yet miles and miles away, the Angel of Death had descended from the Heavens and now stood over my Sarah Sue. I know she knew he was there, because she had invited him into her bedroom. She could have sold her soul to the Devil in exchange for the easing of her pain, but instead she invited Death Angel.

As a Catholic, I am terrified of the Faustian pact with Mephistopheles. How easy would it have been to pray to the Devil to learn how to pick a guitar, instead of sitting under my window night after night figuring it out the good old-fashioned way? The former costs you your soul and the later earns your way into Heaven.

Had I known that Death Angel stood in her room preparing to take her away, I would have sold my soul to the Devil on the spot, without any hesitation. That would be quite the predicament, wouldn't it? I'd've signed a pact with the Devil and she's made a deal with Death Angel. Whose contract would take precedence in the Heavenly Courts?

I would never find out the answer to that question.

Sarah Sue had already taken that bottle of pills and washed them down with whiskey stolen from her old man's liquor cabinet. Is it poetic or ironic that the whiskey that fueled her father's anger, hatred, and violence is the same bottle in which Sarah Sue would finally find her peace.

As a God-fearing Catholic, I know that Sarah Sue will not welcomed into Heaven but ultimately would be punished in Dante's particular and peculiar version and vision of Hell. It is in the Inferno's Wood of the Suicides where Sarah Sue would be transformed into gnarled and ensnarled bushes and trees, only to have hideous Harpies make their nests in her. This is where my soul believes she will spend eternity.

But my heart, cannot help but believe that we will have our eternity together in the peace and serenity of Heaven. What was stolen from us on this Earth will be restored in Eternity.

Until then, I have a few questions for Death Angel:

Buddy:

From the Album
Death Angel, Death Angel,
Why did you answer her call?
Death Angel, Death Angel,
I'd have been there if she should fall.
I'd have washed her scraped knee.
I'd have done anything she needed of me.

Death Angel, Death Angel,
Why did you walk into her home.

Death Angel, Death Angel,
Couldn't you have left her alone?
I'd have nursed her through her pain,
The sun would've shone through the rain.

Death Angel, Death Angel,
Did you stand there when she slit her wrists?
Death Angel, Death Angel,
Couldn't have you crossed her name off your list?
Couldn't you leave her alone with me?
Couldn't you leave her be?

Death Angel, Death Angel,
You took the only girl I'll love.
Death Angel, Death Angel,
I know you serve the One Above.
But let Him know that starting tonight,
I'll never ever again be all right.

Death Angel, Death Angel,
You won't see me for a long time.
Death Angel, Death Angel,
You see I haven't committed a crime.
Except the crime of loving someone.
My life isn't over… in fact, it's just begun.

The Healing Does Come

"Welcome, back to the Malt Shop Hour," said Soda Jerk Perkins, "you have been listening to the recently rereleased 50's classic *I Was A Teenage Angel of Death* by Buddy Brown. It has been a nice walk down memory lane to that bygone era of young love, in his case, unrequited love. During the last hour, I hope that you have laughed and cried with Buddy Brown and Sarah Sue.

"Buddy, I can't imagine the pain that Sarah Sue's death caused a young man just preparing to live his life only to have death come into it so quickly and so mercilessly."

"At first, her death made my heart hurt with every breath, every beat of my heart pulsed not only blood through my body, but stirred memories throughout my mind. It was relentless," I said.

"I came very close to killing myself. I dreamed of being gnarled and ensnarled with my

Sarah Sue in the Wood of Suicides, so that we would have our eternity together. But only the dreadful thought of Satan gnarling and ensnarling us just out of reach of each other spared my hand and my life.

"As each day turned into a week, into a month, and into years, the pain faded into memory and the memories were transformed into song. It was through the finishing of those songs written under my window that gave my life a purpose. I transformed each pain into a note and those notes into songs."

"That must have been cathartic," Soda Jerk said.

"It was pleasantly cathartic. One wouldn't think that exposing one's emotions to the world would ease the pain. Where some drown themselves in drink, I wrote and sang my songs.

"But God does ease the pain each and every day. This is what Sarah Sue could not see and could not understand. She believed that the pain caused by Johnny Angel's death would hurt that bad every day for the rest of her life. While I'm sure there are pains that never seem to subside, like the death of a child, but most pain blessedly wanes instead of waxing forever and ever."

"But I had chosen to live with the pain of Sarah Sue's death. I chose not to end my life, which would have been easy, far too easy. I drew strength from the pain, instead of running away from it. I chose to write songs about Sarah Sue. I chose to remember Sarah Sue. I chose to honor Sarah Sue by living my life. She would have wanted me to find a nice woman and settle down with a brood of children. She may not have been there to be their Godmother, but she, I pray, became their Guardian Angel."

From the Album

Buddy: *When you least except it, the healing does come,*
You'll never find it in a bottle of Jamaican rum.
When you least except it, God shines his light.
All the pains disappears and everything is all right.

The healing does come,
When you feel numb.
The healing does come,
With each rising of the sun.

I'll feel the pain of my little Sarah Sue's death,
Until the day I breathe my very last breath.
But God eases the pain a little bit each day.
When the pain will be gone, I hope God'll never say.

The healing does come,
When you feel numb.
The healing does come,
With each rising of the sun.

You need the pain of that death in your heart,
As a constant reminder that you'll never be apart.
That Sarah Sue will be with me until the end,
That Sarah Sue is not gone. She is still my best friend.

The healing does come,
When you feel numb.
The healing does come,
With each rising of the sun.

Like It Was Yesterday (Reprise)

"And when I least expected it, I found true love. I remember it like it was yesterday.

"After graduation (I graduated for the sake of my parents), I hitched my way to New York like Sarah Sue would have wanted me to and my songs found their way into the ears of record producers. They would hone them into radio-friendly hits. A label would then press the vinyl and put me out on the road. The songs had also found their way into the heart of a young lady, who happened to be the singer who sang as Sarah Sue immortally on wax."

"Sarah Sue became Sarah Sue?" Soda Jerk asked.

"I had been singing the songs that would eventually become *I Was A Teenage Angel of Death* at open mic nights. Some nights, I would only get to sing one or two songs, some others a few more. I don't believe anybody at the bars and coffee shops had any idea that the songs I sang told a story. They had no clue who this Sarah Sue was. Nobody did.

"Until I noticed a certain young lady kept appearing whenever I performed. She would be there and then she wouldn't be there. One night after singing a couple of songs, she bought me a drink and inquired who this Sarah Sue was that I always sung so passionately about. She inquired if were there more songs than I was able to sing about her. After the bar closed, we retreated to my apartment. I told her the story and sang her the songs. She sat on the couch in my apartment and cried.

"She wanted to know why I sang Sarah Sue's verses and choruses and I told her I didn't have any other voice other than my own. And she soon began to stand beside me on the stage and brought Sarah Sue back to life. Sarah Sue would find her immortality in this attractive and spirited young woman. Buddy Brown would find true and enduring love in this attractive and spirited young woman. I couldn't have my first Sarah Sue, through some twist of fate, I was able to love and make love to my second Sarah Sue.

"I had a life and a family.

"Would I have written *I Was A Teenage Angel of Death* if Sarah Sue had lived? Would I have left our small town if Sarah Sue was alive? Would have I met my wife and the mother of my children if Sarah Sue hadn't chosen to do what she did? This is where we get into trouble. There is an endless series of what if's that will drive any sane man insane. We cannot dwell on the what if's. We can only live with what happened."

From the Album

Buddy:
The mind is a patchwork of yesterdays
One by one they will soon decay.
They all seem to blur together,
And blow away into the ether.

I cried and cried for what seems like years.
I couldn't stop, just couldn't stop the tears.
I felt like, just left like I had been cursed.

But my life changed when things were the worst.

I no longer think of Sarah Sue Hayes,
(But when I do…)
All the years seem to fade into days.
Back when the future was a distant someday.
Ah, I remember it like it was yesterday.

There was a time when my life hit the skids.
Then I met my wife and we had a few kids.
I'd have been happy with Sarah Sue as my wife.
But then again, that would have been another life.

I no longer think of Sarah Sue Hayes,
(But when I do…)
All the years seem to fade into days.
Back when the future was a distant someday.
Ah, I remember it like it was yesterday.

The mind is a patchwork of yesterdays
One by one they will soon decay.
They all seem to blur together,
And blow away into the ether.

The End

Author's Note: I have always been fascinated by concept albums and "Rock" Operas. From The Who's *Tommy* to *Beethoven's Last Night* by Trans-Siberian Orchestra, I have been addicted to collecting these types of albums in any and all genres of music. My love for Rock Operas inspired me to write my own. Beginning with the Faustian pact between Robert Johnson and the Devil, I wrote the story and libretto to a Blues Opera I called *Satan's Preacher Man*. After finding the perfect Blues guitarist, a man named Rick Terlep, who would write the music to our Blues Opera, and drawing singers from the various local theatre companies I have worked with over the years, we recorded our own concept album, *Satan's Preacher Man*, a Blues Opera. After pressing the 30 song double-disk album, I then set off on the journey towards my next Rock Opera.

This journey would take me far and wide. From traditional songs like "Frankie and Albert" to the strange, twisted fad of teenage tragedy (or "teen death") songs from the 1950's, where I would find my deepest inspiration. Songs like Jody Reynolds' "Endless Sleep", Mark Dinning's "Teen Angel", Ray Peterson's "Tell Laura I Love Her", and J. Frank Wilson and the Cavaliers' cover of "Last Kiss" planted the seed of an album-length Rock Opera based around a fateful relationship. Due to life's circumstances, the lyrics to my Rock Opera, unfortunately, languished without music in the bowels of my computer for a great number of years. The successful publication of my novels would lead me down a different, more literary path. I'd turn the lyrics of what I would soon call *I Was A Teenage Angel of Death* into the young adult, coming-of-age novel you hold in your hands.

www.ingramcontent.com/pod-product-compliance
Lightning Source LLC
Chambersburg PA
CBHW080726280626
47162CB00020B/3089